ELEMENTS OF THE **EXTRAORDINARY**

Face Reading

Can you face the facts?

Other books in the Elements of the Extraordinary series:

Do-it-yourself Feng Shui – Take charge of your destiny!
ESP – Are you a mind-reader?
Prophecies – Can you see into the future?
Handwriting – Can you read your character?
Tea leaves, herbs, and flowers – Fortune-telling the Gypsy way
Hand Reading – Discover your future

ELEMENTS OF THE **EXTRAORDINARY**

Face Reading

Can you face the facts?

Wu Ying

Illustrated by Paul Davies

ELEMENT
CHILDREN'S BOOKS

SHAFTESBURY, DORSET · BOSTON, MASSACHUSETTS · MELBOURNE, VICTORIA

For Ding Ru-Chang

First published in Great Britain 1998 by
Element Children's Books
Shaftesbury, Dorset SP7 8BP

Published in the USA 1998 by
Element Books, Inc.
160 North Washington Street, Boston MA 02114

Published in Australia 1998 by
Element Books and distributed by
Penguin Australia Limited,
487 Maroondah Highway, Ringwood, Victoria 3134

Cover photography: Jon Stone
Cover design: Ness Wood

British Library Cataloguing in Publication data available.
Library of Congress Cataloging in Publication data available.

1 901881 87 3

Typeset by Dorchester Typesetting Group Ltd
Printed and bound in Great Britain by
Creative Print and Design

Contents

CHAPTER 1

Fun With Feng

The air was full of good *qi* (pronounced chee). That's the invisible energy you feel zipping about all over the place on a really lovely day. I just had to go out and enjoy it. You know what I mean, it wasn't too hot, it wasn't too cold – it was one of those days when you're happy to be alive, soaking up the sun, stretching your legs and smelling the flowers.

Not that I actually smelled the flowers, of course. I didn't skip around the park like some nutcase, sniffing plants and singing songs. But I did sit down on a bench to read a book. And, because I'm a *feng shui* (pronounced *fung shway*) master in training, I made sure I found the right sort of bench. Far away from the kids playing football, because the last thing I needed was a ball bouncing off my head every ten seconds. Out of direct sunlight, but away from any overhanging branches that might cast distracting shadows. There were a couple of girls with kites nearby, but they didn't look as if they'd be any trouble. That's what feng shui is all about – making sure that you can make the best of wherever you are. It keeps you calm, in harmony with nature, and very brainy.

So finally, because a feng shui master takes his time getting everything just right, I leaned back and started to read.

"What's that?" The voice beside me belonged to a strange-looking old lady with a fan. She wafted it slowly back and forth in front of her face and stared right into my eyes.

"A book," I mumbled.

"Good, is it?" she asked.

"This particular bit," I said carefully, "was especially interesting, until I was interrupted."

The birds tweeted softly in the trees. Distant yells and thumps from the football game told me that someone was disagreeing with the referee. The girls' kites twisted in the breeze. The mad-eyed old lady whisked her fan around for a bit. I could tell she was still looking at me. Maybe I should just get up and walk off, I thought.

"Your great-grandmother says *hello*," said the old lady, quietly.

"What did you say?"

"*Hello*. From your great-grandmother."

"How do you know her?"

"She's very pleased with your improvement at school," she continued.

"I asked you a question," I said.

"Yes, dear," she said briskly. "And when I asked you one a moment ago, all I got was the cold shoulder."

"Er, sorry," I said.

"I should hope so, too." She sniffed, absently opening and shutting the fan. "You took one look at me and thought I was a pickpocket or a tramp, didn't you?"

"Er..."

"You sat there and thought to yourself, "Oh goody, a loonie. I'd better run for it before she starts telling me some never ending story, didn't you?"

"How did you know that?"

"Because," she hissed, "I can read you like a book. I can see it in your face. I know your character, your personality, your attitude to life. Everything."

"Really?"

"Oh, yes. No point in keeping your thoughts to yourself, you might as well broadcast them to the world through a loudspeaker."

"Why?"

"Because I can read your face," she said. "And it tells me about you and your future."

"Hang on," I said. "You can't predict the future—"

"But you can change it, right?" she interrupted. "Yes, yes, I know all about feng shui and all that," she said. "And you ought to know by now that it's a bad idea for a level one, Z-grade, private-first-class grunt of a feng shui master to try and second-guess his elders and betters."

"Are you a sorcerer?" I ventured meekly.

"Just thank your lucky stars I'm not a dragon in disguise," she snapped. "I would have had you toasted for dinner."

"But what was that about being able to see into the future?" I asked. "You can't use feng shui to tell fortunes."

"Of course not," she said. "You use common sense." She snapped her fan shut and held it over her head. "What happens if I let go?" she said.

"It'll fall," I replied.

She dropped the fan with a smile, and it tumbled towards the ground. Halfway down, it snapped open and wafted sideways like a kite, back into her other hand.

"How about that?"

"A gust of wind," I said, trying to sound unimpressed.

"Yes," she said. "But if you'd known it was coming, your eyes wouldn't have bulged out of their sockets like that. I knew it was coming because I kept my eye on the girls over there. Their kites twirled three seconds earlier in the same gust of wind."

"So…?"

"So, I knew it would happen. I just predicted the future, and I did it by keeping my eye on what was happening in the present. Just as your face tells me about you now, and gives me hints about you in the future."

"Just like a kite in the wind?"

"Sort of."

"So," she said. "Let's try again. Good, is it?"

"What?"

"That book."

The book was now hanging limply in my hand. I couldn't even remember what page I was on.

"You can call me Aunty Feng," she said with a smile.

"Feng?" I said. "As in feng shui?"

"Er... no, not exactly," she replied. "It's a different kind of feng."

"Oh," I said, which is always a good response when you don't understand what's going on.

"The words might sound the same to you," she went on, "but there are all kinds of different meanings which only Chinese people can spot."

"I am Chinese!" I said, feeling slightly hurt.

"Of course you are, dear," she said, giving me a kindly pat on the hand. "It's just that you still haven't learned all the different tones. You have to sing Chinese when you speak it, otherwise it just sounds like gibberish."

"Oh," I said. "OK."

"So," she said, "we've got *feng* meaning *wind*, *feng* meaning *plentiful*, *feng* meaning *bonfire*, *feng* meaning *mad as a spoon*, oh... lots of different *fengs*." Every time she said the word, it sounded ever so slightly different. My parents didn't speak Chinese to each other so I'd never really had to listen to it before. It all sounded very confusing.

"And which feng are you?" I asked. "Are you Aunty Bonfire? Or maybe you're Aunty Mad?"

"Oh, no," she said with a chuckle. "I'm another kind of Feng altogether."

"If you say so," I mumbled. She looked to me like a prime candidate for Aunty Mad.

CHAPTER 2

Color Me Bad

"How much do you know about feng shui?" she asked.

"Loads," I said, modestly.

"Well, face reading is like doing feng shui on your head," said Aunty Feng. "You have to decide which parts are lucky and which parts are unlucky. The difference is that you can't change your face but you can change your fate. We use face reading to look at a person's character, and feng shui to change it."

"Ooh, cool!"

"Glad you think so," she said. "See, you can judge a book by its cover, after all."

"Am I a good book?" I asked.

"Well, you're not a bad book," she said. "You're quite enthusiastic and active, but I can see there are a few parts of your character you need to work on."

"Like what?"

"Like arrogance, pride, and impatience."

"Oh."

"The Chinese place great value on face, because your face is the mask you turn to the outside world. If someone has a *big face* they are a bit of a show-off. Like you."

"Oh, sorry."

"That's all right, dear. Most face reading is all about measurements and shapes, checking out the different features on someone's face. We'll start by looking at their skin, to work out which element rules them. There are five Chinese elements, so there are five types of character you have to look for."

"That should be pretty easy," I said.

"Why?" said Aunty Feng.

"Well, it's not like the color of someone's face is a secret, is it? Elements must be easy to spot."

"All right, then," said Aunty Feng. "If you think you're so smart, give it a try."

"Well," I said. "In feng shui there are five elements, right?"

"Right."

"And they are Fire, Water, Wood, Metal, and Earth. Right?"

"OK so far," said Aunty Feng, examining her fingernails.

"And each element has a color. Fire is red, Water is black or blue, Wood is green, Metal is white, and Earth is yellow. Right?"

"Keep going," said Aunty Feng, mysteriously.

"So, it's easy. White people are Metal, Black people are Water, Yellow people are Earth, and Red people are Fire."

"I see," said Aunty Feng. "What about Wood? What people are Wood?"

"Er... people with green skin...?" I ventured.

"No!" said Aunty Feng, slapping me around the ear with her fan. "No! No! No! Are all native Americans fiery?"

"Er... no."

"Are all white people rich?"

"Er… no."

"Are all black people wet?"

"Er—"

"Well, that's what you're saying, dear! You're trying to tell me that everybody with the same skin color will act exactly the same, aren't you?"

"Er… yes."

"But it isn't true, is it?"

"Er... no."

"Because what does that make you? You're half Chinese and half barbarian. So what are you?"

"A bit of Metal and a bit of Earth?" I suggested, feeling a little silly.

"What? Like a muddy old coin?" Aunty Feng shook her head fiercely. "What color is white skin?"

"Is this a trick question?" I asked timidly.

"What color is white skin?" she said sternly, whisking her fan faster as if to blow me out of my seat.

"White skin is white," I said with a shrug.

"Is it?"

"Well, sort of pinky-white," I said. "Unless it's tanned, in which case it's more like brown. Or if someone's angry, then it goes red."

"That's more like it," said Aunty Feng. "Keep going."

"It might go blue if you're really cold. Or green if you're ill."

"And black skin?"

"Is kind of brown, really," I said. "Sometimes it can be so black that it looks almost bluey, but some black people have really light skin, lighter than some white people with tans."

"Now," said Aunty Feng, "you're thinking like a sorcerer."

Skin Deep

It doesn't matter what color you are, your ruling element is determined by the *hue* of your skin. Whether you are Chinese or Nigerian, Mexican or Norwegian, your skin will not be easily described by a single color. The single color, black, white, red, yellow, or brown, is your race, but the way in which your skin differs ever so slightly from the basic color will tell you what your ruling element is.

Skin has no color on its own, but can be any shade from white to black depending on the pigment in it, which is called melanin. Very pale white people have very little melanin. Very dark black people have lots of melanin. People who are in between are browner or yellower.

The color of your skin is also influenced by the blood underneath it. If the blood is close to the surface in large amounts, it will make your skin redder. The veins beneath the surface or the cold outside can make it bluer. That's a

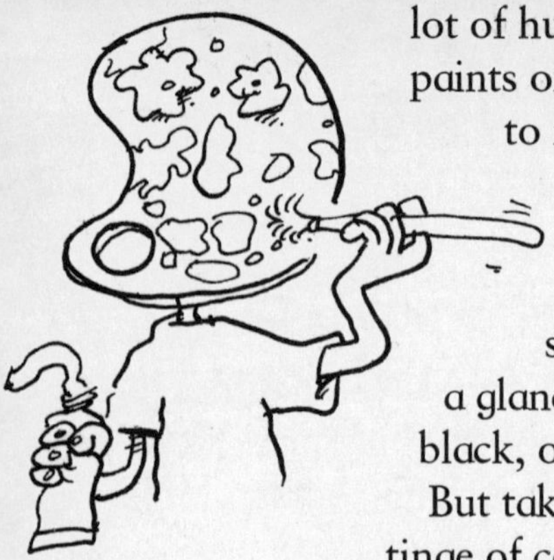

lot of hues to play with. If those were paints on a palette you would be able to mix and match them to make almost any other color you can think of. That's why we can't talk in terms of straightforward skin color. At a glance, someone will appear to be black, or white, or yellow, or brown. But take a closer look. It's that extra tinge of color we want to find, because that indicates the ruling element.

You may find this quite difficult to do at first, so get a few of your friends together and compare them. The more faces you can look at while you're reading this book, the easier it will be for you to see some of the tiny differences that can be so important. But a word of warning: it's better to compare the faces of your friends rather than those of your family. This is because you and your family will probably share a lot of the same characteristics, so you won't see so many obvious differences. You might have exactly the same skin color, the same nose, eyes, or mouth, and so on. Don't try reading your family's faces until you've practiced for a while on people to whom you are not related. It'll be easier with them to spot a greenish tinge to the skin, a big nose, or small ears.

Get Your Light Right

You will need a mirror if you are trying this on yourself. Don't just guess the color of your face by looking at your hands, because they will probably be a slightly different color. Whether you try this on yourself or on a friend, make sure you are somewhere with natural light. Fluorescent lights, tinted light bulbs, or even rooms painted a strong color can all give your face a slightly different tone, and you will want to see its real color.

Fire

A reddish tinge to someone's skin means they will be ruled by the element Fire. Active, and dynamic, the fiery person is a good choice for a leader, and is a hard-working soul. Although if they ever get out of control you may have trouble keeping them down. Fiery people must beware of dry skin and sore throats, but also of overindulgence and hot temper. The skin of the face goes red when someone is overheated or angry, so the fiery person must take care that they don't do so much running around that they exhaust themselves, or get so concerned about something that they blow a fuse. They should aim to keep calm and cool at all costs.

Water

If someone's skin is so pale that the veins show through, or so black that it has a kind of bluey glow, it is a sign that they are ruled by Water. The watery person is sensitive and changeable, prone to deep thought and quiet intellectual activities. The Water person must beware of runny noses, catarrh, phlegm, and earache, all of which can come about through their overly wet nature. Just as black areas in the skin mean that someone is easily bruised, the feelings of a Water person are easily hurt. Like the sea, all forms of water can be unpredictable, and the Water person must sometimes be reminded not to take things too seriously. Otherwise, they can blow up like a storm, and throw their friends around like little fishing boats.

Wood

This is the rarest ruling element to find, because it requires a fair amount of blue and yellow before it can appear. Nevertheless, if you find that one person in a trillion who appears to have a greenish tinge to their skin, be they black, white, brown, or yellow by birth, then you've found someone who is ruled by the element Wood. The Wood person is slow but sure, happy to let the other creatures run around the forest and play in their branches while they

grow and flourish, pushing ever onwards and upwards. In the famous race between the hare and the tortoise (which is a story the Chinese have too), the tortoise is the Wood character, plodding ever on and eventually overtaking the quitters who were originally so quick off the mark. Wood people are quiet, confident, and modest, because they know they will eventually be the tallest in the forest if they are left to their own devices. They must be careful that their joints and feet (roots) do not become brittle and easily snapped off for firewood. Someone whose face indicates a Wood element may find that others are taking advantage of them, so they should beware of doing too many favors for others.

Metal

If your skin is very, very pale compared with that of other members of your race, then you are ruled by the Metal element. Metal people are focused and strong, cutting like knives through any obstacles that get in their way. Once they make up their minds, they are very difficult to dissuade, and their strong links with money make them very astute in financial matters. Minerals and vitamins are very important for the health of the Metal person; they must make sure they never run low on any of these if they want to stay fit. They must be careful that their sharp wits do not hurt others who are not as strong as themselves. The Metal person risks being a little thoughtless towards others, and may need to be reminded that all that glitters is not gold.

Earth

People with skin that is brown or yellowish in its hue are ruled by the Earth. Strong and reliable, such a person is often the most trusted and respected one in a circle of friends. Like the ground on which we all stand, earthy people are supportive to the last. Their weak points healthwise are likely to be in the *rocks* of the body, the bones that hold everything up. Earth people must be careful that they don't become too stubborn or set in their ways. Like Wood people who are similarly rooted to the spot, they can run the risk of being a stick-in-the-mud. Earth people may be reliable and able to put up with all manner of minor annoyances like tilling the soil and mining, but ultimately, they may snap in a terrible fit of temper. Their friends should pay extra special attention to their feelings, because Earth people will not give any warnings when something is making

them angry. Instead, they will suddenly crack open in a terrible quake, and woe betide whoever has caused the explosion.

Face Value

- ☺ No matter what color your skin is supposed to be, you should be able to see a tinge of another color in it.
- ☺ This tinge is caused by your ruling element, which could be Fire, Water, Wood, Metal, or Earth.
- ☺ Make sure you look for the tinge of color in natural lighting, and on your face not your hands or armpits! This is a book about *face* reading, not foot reading!

Face Facts: Ruling Elements

FACE HUE	ELEMENT	CHARACTERISTICS
Reddish	Fire	Hot-tempered, flustered
Blue/Black	Water	Sensitive, intellectual
Greenish	Wood	Slow but sure
White/Pale	Metal	Focused, sharp
Yellow/Brown	Earth	Reliable, strong

Face to Face

This is the first *Face to Face* section. Aunty Feng has put it in to make sure you're paying attention. And there will be more later.

Someone in the house has broken a vase, and there are two suspects standing in front of you. Neither of them will admit to it, but only one of them is lying. One has healthy, normal-looking skin on her face, but the other one is

slowly going redder and redder. Which one is most likely to be telling the truth?

Thank you so much. I told you this would be easy. Just as Nature paints black and yellow stripes on wasps and bees to let us know they're dangerous, it likes to paint colors on people's faces so that others can find out more about them. That's why teachers always seem to know who threw what. Your face gives you away.

CHAPTER 3

Hearing Things

"I know what you're thinking," said Aunty Feng.

"You do?!"

"You're thinking all this is rather obvious."

I thought it was best to be honest. If she knew my every thought, there was no point in lying.

"It's obvious now you've told me," I said. "I mean, I'd never thought about it before, but since you've mentioned it, my face is kind of pinker than everyone else's. And I can be a little bit hot-tempered now and then. But surely that's not all there is to it, and to ME?"

"Of course not," said Aunty Feng. "Every single feature on the face tells us something about you and your fate. We just have to go through each one until we have built up a list."

"Where do we start?" I asked.

"Well, since you're a kid, we ought to start with the ears."

"My ears?"

"Oh, yes, they stick out like little radar dishes, don't they?"

"And that's good is it?"

"Could be," said Aunty Feng.

The Good Ear

To read somebody's ears, you must face them straight-on and check what part of the face is level with the top and bottom of the ear. The perfect Chinese ear will have a top that is level with the bottom of the eyebrows, and an ear lobe that is level with the base of the nose. Someone with ears that fit this description will be honest, kind, and a good friend. If the ears are too small, the possessor may be a trifle shy or unassuming. Large ears are a sign of a good heart and a fortunate future.

If the top tip of the ear extends above the browline, you might be a little selfish. Although you may do well in your chosen profession, you may do so at the expense of others. If the bottom of the ear extends below the base of the nose, it is a sign of great success late in life.

Shape of Ears

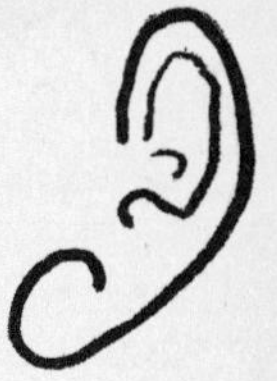

There are four main shapes of ear, and each tells you more information about someone's character. A rectangular ear is the most common type. Taller than it is wide, it has a regular width all the way up. Because this type of ear is so common, it signifies normality and stability. This is a person you can trust, someone sane, calm, and steadfast.

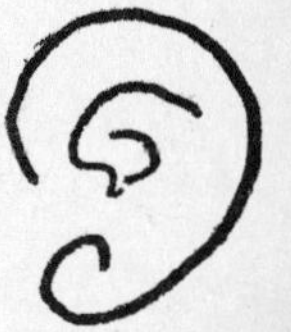

If the top part of the ear is wider than the base, the person has good hearing because the wide upper part works like a radar dish collecting sound. This in turn makes them alert and intuitive. They are often able to hear things before others do, and this carries over into other areas of life. Someone with top-heavy ears is likely to come up with ideas faster than their friends, and will be very good at thinking on their feet or, if you like, thinking on their ears. They are also difficult to fool, because they can hear the quaver in your voice when you lie to them.

An ear that is wider at the base than at the top is a sign of great wisdom and a long, long life. It also shows that the possessor likes to look before he leaps, and is liable to sit and think about any major decision, tugging thoughtfully at his long ear lobes. Unlike owners of the top-heavy ears, the owners of bottom-heavy ears will often take a long time to reach a decision; perhaps too long.

If the ear is rounder, almost circular rather than rectangular

or irregular, then the possessor is very creative. Round ears can be found on many artists and writers, and are a sign of a great love of culture, literature, or music. But they signify a certain dizziness when it comes to business and other practical matters.

Position of Ears

If your ears stick out like the wings of a butterfly, you are fated to be as lighthearted and carefree as one of these insects. You also run the risk of being blown about by the winds of fortune, and devoting too much time to enjoying yourself when you should be preparing for the end of summer and the beginning of the long, cold winter.

If your ears are pinned back close to your head like those of a nervous horse, you will be prudent and sensible, but will risk being so cautious that you never actually get around to doing anything.

Color of Ears

Whatever the color of your skin, your ears should be a shade lighter if you are to have a perfect face fortune. If the ears are red, it is a sign that much blood is flowing through them. As usual, this means embarrassment or a hot temper. Someone with red ears is likely to be rash and impetuous. If the ears are also dry and flaky, it is a sign of unbalanced energy. Something in the person's character is sapping all their energy, making them unable to deal with human relationships – a very bad choice as a boyfriend or girlfriend.

If the ears are not reddish, but actually *darker* than the skin on the face, it indicates someone who is easily impressed, and who needs to raise the goals in their life.

The Wheels of Fortune

There are three parts to the ear: the *outer wheel* around the edge, the *inner wheel* formed by the ridge on the inside, and the *lobe* which is that dangly bit at the bottom. If the outer wheel is thick and fleshy, it is a sign of an earthy, physical person who is ruled by the body, not by the mind. Beware of overindulgence, and watch out for tantrums; the chances are high that this person was spoiled as a child by their parents.

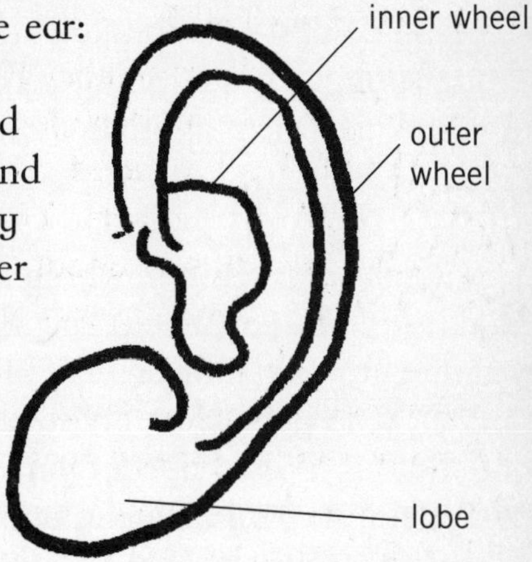

If the outer wheel is thin and sharp, like the edge of a knife, it means the owner is quick-witted and shrewd. The thin edges of their ears make them razor sharp, and they are fast-thinking people, likely to keep their cool whilst everybody else is panicking.

If the outer wheel is pointed, you are looking at the rare Elf's Ear, a sign of a truly mysterious person. The owner of an Elf's Ear may be a genuinely nice person, but don't expect them to understand everything you say or do, because their way of thinking is very different from everybody else's. As long as you understand each other, you'll get on fine, but just remember that if they do anything you think of as nasty or spiteful, they honestly might not have thought about your feelings. Tell them what you're thinking, and give them another chance.

The Inner Wheel

The inner wheel is the little spiral of cartilage on the inside of the human ear, encircling the ear hole. If it sticks out prominently, it indicates a highly sociable and friendly person, who is both outgoing and easygoing. If it is smaller and flatter it is a sign of an introvert who likes to stay away from crowds, bustle, and noise; a quiet person who doesn't talk much. If the hole that leads to the inner ear itself is large and wide, it is a sign of a person who listens to a wide range of opinions, and is a good sign that the person is open-minded and prepared to consider new ideas.

The Dangly Bit

The ear lobe is an important indicator of wisdom and of long life. Although a fat outer wheel is a bad sign, a fat lobe is a good one! The longer and fatter the ear lobe, the longer your life will be. Some people are born without dangly bits on their ears, but this doesn't mean they are going to die young, it just means they shouldn't expect to live to attend their hundredth birthday party. They tend to make up for it by ensuring they have something really major to celebrate at all the other parties. They are bright, bubbly, and sociable, and love going to parties.

Some ear lobes do not swing freely, but are attached to the side of the head by a small flap of skin. These attached lobes are a sign of the artful dodger – a person who can always look after number one, and who never fails to come up smelling of roses, whatever they may have stepped in.

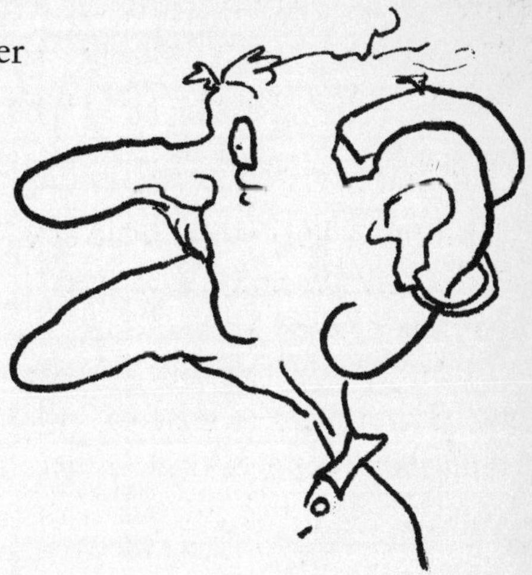

As people get older, their ear lobes often grow longer. This is because the lobe is also a sign of wisdom, and people will naturally get wiser as they get older.

Face Value

- ☺ The ear is divided into three parts, the inner wheel, the outer wheel, and the lobe.
- ☺ Ears are like radar for collecting sound, and gathering opinions. The bigger the ears, the more open you are to hearing the thoughts of others.
- ☺ Small ears are a sign that you'd rather not listen to others. You want to make up your own mind, or perhaps you just don't care what other people think!

Face Facts: Ears

EAR FEATURE	CHARACTERISTIC
Level with brow (top) and nostril (bottom)	Normal
Tip above brow	Selfish but successful
Base below nostril	Success in later life
Large	Good fortune and good heart
Small	Shy and unassuming
Lighter coloring than face	Good fortune
Redder than face	Hot-tempered
Darker than face	Easily impressed
Flaky skin	Bad in relationships
Fat outer wheel	Spoiled
Thin outer wheel	Shrewd and cunning
Pointy, elfin ear	Mysterious
Inner wheel sticks out	Outgoing, extrovert
Inner wheel is flattened	Shy, introvert
Large ear hole	Open mind
Small ear hole	Closed mind
Long lobe	Long life and wisdom
Lobe attached to side of head	Cunning
Ears stick out	Flighty like a butterfly
Ears pinned back	Nervous like a scared horse

Face to Face

You need someone to keep a look out while you set a childish (yet somehow very satisfying) trap in your sister's bedroom. As you look across the assembled gang of your friends, you have to decide who will be best at the job. Obviously, the bigger the ears, the better they will be at hearing her approach, but three of your friends have ears the same size. Friend (A) has huge ears that stick out for miles. Friend (B) has ears that extend below the level of his nostrils, and Friend (C) has big ears that are pinned back to the side of his head. Which one would you choose?

CHAPTER 4

Brow Beating

"I see," I said. "You're deliberately trying to catch me out."

"How's that?" asked Aunty Feng.

"Well," I said with a flourish, "Friend (A) might have radar ears, but they're also butterfly ears. If you put him on watch he might end up looking the wrong way. Low-flying ears mean success in later life, which is all very well but it means Friend (B) is no use to me."

"Very good," agreed Aunty Feng. "Be very wary of putting too much faith in other people's good fortune. Just because their face reading says they'll be lucky, it doesn't follow that their luck will rub off on you. Good fortune for them might be that they're out of town when you're arrested."

"Friend (C)," I went on, "is as jumpy and nervous as a thoroughbred horse. He won't just scream and holler a warning when my sister comes up the path, he'll yell the place down if he sees a cat, a dog, or even a worm that might just be wriggling in his direction."

"That's right," said Aunty Feng. "But he's the best choice out of the three, and you'll just have to put up with a few false alarms."

"Is that it?" I asked.

"Is what what?" she said.

"Surely there must be a way of finding out if he really is the best choice."

"Of course there is," said Aunty Feng. "That's why people have more than one feature on their face. I'm just trying to keep things simple until you've got the idea."

"I see," I smiled, raising a cunning eyebrow like a baddie in the movies.

Aunty Feng snickered behind her fan.

"I love the way you do that," she said.

"Do what?"

"The whole eyebrow-raising thing. I never could manage it."

"I never really thought about it," I said. "I just do it."

"Trust me," said Aunty Feng, "not everybody can. But take care the wind doesn't change or you may find yourself stuck that way."

"That doesn't happen," I said. "Does it?"

Talking Eyebrows

The Chinese have always been fascinated by something they call *brow language*, which is the ability of many Westerners to communicate by raising their eyebrows. Both eyebrows raised mean surprise, a single eyebrow raised means disbelief, and both brows furrowed mean intense worry or consternation. Chinese people can move their eyebrows too, but don't get so much practice. For them, the face is supposed to be a mask to the outside world, so the last thing they want is for their mask to have neon signs plastered over it advertising that they're worried, shocked, or don't believe what someone is saying. In ancient China, the ladies of the court were so worried about giving away their feelings that they gave themselves *Moth brows*. This meant shaving off their eyebrows and painting false ones halfway up their forehead where they were less likely to move around.

Eyebrows in face reading are tied up with a person's wisdom. As the saying goes, the longer the eyebrows, the wiser the person. That's why you often see statues of beetle-browed old men in Chinese temples or restaurants. The great Chinese philosopher and teacher Confucius (551–479 BC) is often depicted with big, bushy eyebrows and a tufty beard (another sign of wisdom). Eyebrows that are shorter in length than the eye below them can be signs of misfortune in later life, as are messy, uneven brows or brows that sit, caveman-style, too close to the eyes themselves.

Fortunate Eyebrows

Moon brows are shaped like little lunar crescents turned sideways above the eyes. People with Moon brows are like the moon itself, associated with changeability and deep emotions, but also with extreme cleverness. The moon does not shine with its own light but reflects the light of the sun. Just like the moon itself, people with Moon brows can benefit from associating with bright and talented people; they work well with them by complementing their *sun*. The moon may use the sun's light but turns it into something new and different, which is why people with moon brows often make good actors or musicians. Actors need scripts and musicians need composers but, to tell the truth, both sets of people need each other just as the sun and the moon do.

If the curve is not quite so pronounced, and the brow is wide all the way around, a bit like a segment of orange, this is a *Lion brow*. If you have a Lion brow, you will be happy and lucky, and though you may appear fierce to your enemies, deep down you will just be a big pussycat.

The *Number One* brow is so called because it looks like the Chinese character for *one*, which is like our own number one but turned on its side. Flat, straight and sometimes almost rectangular, the Number One brow indicates someone who has everything under control. It stands for harmony because one and one is two – simple, logical and correct. If you have Number One brows you will always do well.

The *Delicate brow* is long, thin, slightly-curved, and neat. It indicates sophistication and refinement. People with this type of brow will sip tea with their little finger pointing outwards, hold their chopsticks closer to the thick end, bow and curtsey whenever they meet a friendly dragon, and be able to write exquisite, polite, genteel letters. But not all at once, obviously. Delicate brows suggest success in future life, but possibly without having to make much effort. The brows imply that the person is likely to have been born with a silver spoon in their mouth.

The *Tiger brow* is big and well-defined. It looks like one of a tiger's stripes, starting thin, thickening in the middle, then tapering away to a point. Like the tiger itself, this brow signifies a mighty and powerful individual who would prove to be a fierce enemy if provoked. To the Chinese, the tiger was the King of Beasts, and many soldiers in ancient times used to paint the image of a tiger on their shields. If a woman has a Tiger brow, she may be beautiful but also deadly. Watch out for her claws.

But the Tiger was not the most powerful creature just because it was an animal king. The Chinese are not so impressed with kings because they could go one better. They had an Emperor whose crest bore a dragon on it. The *Dragon brow* is straight but points upwards and outwards, so that the two eyebrows on a face look like this: \ /.

Those who have a Dragon brow are bold and heroic, but also lucky and kind. They are born leaders, and are destined to have a long, long life.

Unfortunate Eyebrows

The *Broken brow* is, as the name suggests, one with a gap or bald patch among the hairs. Be careful not to sit absent-mindedly tugging at your eyebrows, because some people's brows won't grow back after being pulled out. If you create a gap in your brow, you may also create a gap in your fortune. Because a bald patch in the eyebrow could be caused by an old battle scar, a person with a Broken brow is like a soldier home from the wars, tough but marked by their experience, and likely to hold a grudge for a long time.

The *Number Eight brow* sits high above the eye, and is shorter in length than the eye itself. The two eyebrows slope upwards towards each other like the roof of a house, creating a quizzical look of permanent surprize, like this: /\. Two lines sloping up to almost meet in the middle is how Chinese people draw the number eight. If you have Number Eight eyebrows, you will be successful, but only after much frustration and hardship. This is because your eyebrows always look like those on the face of a busy man who is wondering how to find enough time to do all his tasks.

Other Bits

If hair grows between the eyebrows, it is called a *Joined brow*. This can be a sign of bad temper and moodiness.

The gap between the eyebrows has it own meaning that can be read from the lines that might appear there as someone gets older. Ask a person to frown and see if lines appear in the gap.

If a single line appears in the middle, it is a sign of good leadership abilities, clear-headedness, and a good, practical way of looking at the world. If two lines appear, it is a sign of someone with a very artistic, creative nature, but also someone who may be prone to being disorganized, and liable to having raging tantrums when they don't get their own way.

Finally, feel the eyebrow itself and see if there is a prominent ridge of bone underneath it. If there is, this is a sign of well-earned fame in later life.

Face Value

- ☺ Regular-shaped eyebrows are good news, especially if they are longer than the eye itself.
- ☺ Short brows, messy, irregular brows, or brows with gaps in them are perhaps less fortunate.
- ☺ Don't just look at the eyebrow itself, feel for the ridge of bone underneath and check the gap in the middle for a complete reading.

Face Facts: Brows

BROW SHAPE	READING
Pointy and curved (Moon)	Emotional, clever
Blunt and curved (Lion)	Lucky, good-hearted
Thin and slightly curved (Delicate)	Beautiful, refined
Straight and horizontal (Number One)	Good organizer
Straight and pointing up in the middle (Number Eight)	Hassled, frustrated
Straight and pointing down in the middle (Dragon)	Fortunate, heroic

Thicker in the middle (Tiger)	Powerful, fierce
Gappy (Broken)	Bitter, badly treated
Joined	Bad tempered
Single line between	Ambitious, practical
Double line between	Artistic, hot-headed
Prominent brow bones	Future fame

Face to Face

A friend comes to you for advice. She has the offer of two part-time jobs to do during the summer vacation and can't make up her mind which one to take. The job in a burger restaurant pays a lot of money and is so close to home she won't have to get up till quite late each morning. There's a low-paid job as a make-up artist in the local theater. It's further away, but it looks like more fun.

Your friend has very dark skin, big, sticky-out butterfly ears, and Moon eyebrows. What advice do you give her? Is she going to enjoy the cut and thrust of the fast-food industry? Is she well-organized enough to impress the restaurant manager into giving her a promotion? Will she excel at repetitive tasks? Or will she prefer to play around with face-paints all day, for hardly any money? What do you think?

CHAPTER 5

Looking Good

"I think I'm getting the hang of this," I said.

"All right," said Aunty Feng. "Answer the question."

"Dark, creative skin, flighty butterfly ears, and dramatic Moon eyebrows. This girl has the theater in her blood, but she couldn't set a microwave timer to save her life. She'll hate serving burgers but she'll love the make-up job, and she stands a good chance of making a career out of it."

"Excellent," said Aunty Feng.

"But I'm a bit worried about all these different things to remember," I said. "It's all getting very complicated."

"It might look that way," said Aunty Feng, "but you'd be surprised how easy it is. Just remember, Some People Can Fly."

"Excuse me?"

"You said it looked complicated. Well, it isn't really. Just

remember **S**ome **P**eople **C**an **F**ly, which stands for *shape*, *position*, *color*, and *features*. Take each part of the face and look at it in each of those ways. That way you won't forget anything important," she said.

"What about eyes?" I complained. "They're different colors, OK, but all eyes are the same shape and in the same place, aren't they?"

"Same shape!?" said Aunty Feng in surprise. "Have you ever opened yours and *looked* at anyone?"

Shape of Eyes

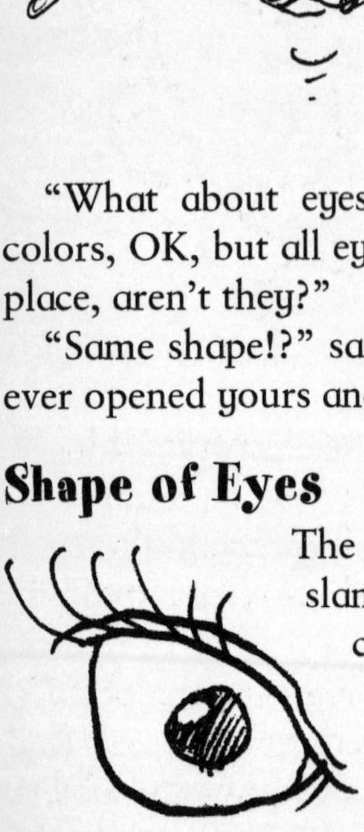

The perfect eye shape is like an almond, slanting up towards the ears. This is called the *Phoenix eye*, and has long been a sign of immense beauty. In ancient China, the Phoenix was the female companion of the Dragon, and a woman with the eyes of this powerful creature was considered a suitable candidate for Empress. But this fortune only works if the rest of the face also denotes kindness, gentleness, and a good heart. If a woman has Phoenix Eyes set in an unfavorable face (for example, with high, flaky ears, or a gappy Tiger brow), then she could be a charming yet unkind person, a temptress or, as they say in the Far East, a woman whose eyes will be the doom of a king.

In men, the same upward-slanting eyes are a sign of greatness, but they are called *Dragon eyes.* These are especially fortunate if combined with *Dragon brows* which also slant upwards and away from the center. If you ever see a performance of Chinese opera, look out for the face of the hero; his make-up will be designed to make his eyes and brows look as dragon-like as possible.

If the eyes slant downwards instead of upwards, it looks as if the person is in pain or holding back tears, so this is a sign of consternation and frustration. The fortune of such people is beset with hardships and bad luck, but they will always pull through in the end.

Large, round eyes signify beauty and kindness, especially because people with big eyes are very expressive, and find it hard to lie convincingly. Because of this powerful ability to express oneself, someone with round eyes is a natural performer, and is likely to enjoy a fortunate career in the arts. If the eyes are too large, however, they make the owner look child-like, and while this itself is often a sign of beauty, it is also a sign of innocence and gullibility. People with large eyes often lack cunning. They are usually good as friends, but they can sometimes have trouble thinking

for themselves. They're too busy waiting to be led by the hand through any problems, and prefer to be followers not leaders. You've probably heard the saying that someone's *eyes are bigger than their stomach*. This comes from a child's inability to understand that it's not possible to fit *all* the food on the table into their mouth. Occasionally you must be firm with large-eyed people, just as you would be with a little child. They genuinely will not realize that they are making a mistake.

On the other hand, people with very small eyes can be very hard to fathom. They are often shy, and even more likely to be single-minded, intense people with very definite aims in life. But because their eyes are too small to see everything in the wide world around them, they sometimes fool themselves into believing they're perfectly happy. They can also be secretive because they are afraid that if they give too much away, more will be taken from them.

Position of Eyes

The position of the eyes is also important for reading someone's character. If they are deep-set in the face, protected by heavy brows, then the person could be a very deep thinker. They are likely to be very smart but also very cautious, preferring to think through every possible angle before starting to do anything. They are good at intellectual games like chess, but often very bad at things like computer games that rely on fast reactions. The ideal job for someone with deep-set eyes is something that involves a lot of thinking, and so they tend to be very rich in later life because they choose big, difficult professions like medicine, law, or languages.

People with deep-set eyes may take their time to reach decisions, but they will usually make the best decision that can be made, so you should always listen to their advice on the rare occasions they offer it.

If someone's eyes are not deep-set but bulge from the head like a frog's, then he or she could also be jumpy and quick off the mark. Eyes that stick out are a sign of a chancer, a gambler, someone with fast reactions, someone who rarely looks before leaping.

Chancers have a great sense of intuition, their reactions are fast, and they are very good at guessing games. But, they also fall for con tricks because they rarely see beneath the surface. People with frog-eyes make great sportsmen and acrobats, but lousy accountants or detectives.

If a person's eyes are close together, they have a very narrow way of looking at the world. They have grown up without noticing what is happening on either side of them because they can only see what it is directly ahead. People with eyes set close together can only see one side to any story. Like a flat flounder fish that has its eyes set close together on the top side only, they seem to flap around on the sea bed, muddling through life and ultimately getting nowhere special. They are likely to need the help of others without realizing that they do. After all, the flounder thinks it is a really smart fish because it lies flat on the sand and pretends to be a rock. But chefs think the flounder is a very useful fish because it has foolishly evolved into a creature that fits snugly into a frying pan. Beware the advice of flounders, because they may not be able to see the fishing hook right in front of their nose.

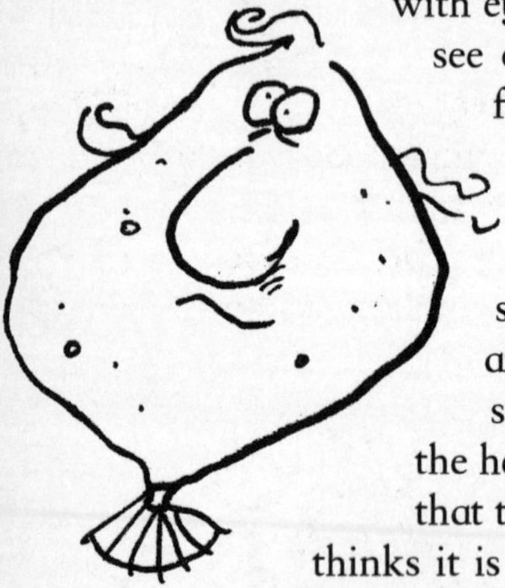

But someone whose eyes are set far apart will be able to see much more of the world around them. Such people will have grown up aware that there is more to life than what they can see in front of them. They will know that others are less fortunate than they are, and because they see so much of the world, they are unable to turn their eyes away. Like the bird that sees so much because its eyes are on opposite sides of its head, such a person will have a very wide perspective on the world. They are likely to be charitable and giving, sometimes too much so because they are often nice to others who do not really deserve their kindness.

Color of Eyes

The most obvious feature of someone's eyes is the color. Asian eyes have quite a small range of colors, and for a long time, Westerners were called *blue-eyed barbarians*. Eventually, when the Chinese looked closer, they discovered that not all foreigners' eyes were blue, and they came up with the following types.

Blue eyes are a sign of a bright, happy personality, and of someone who has trouble lying. No matter what trouble fate may throw in their direction, someone with blue eyes will always pull through in the end and come up smiling, which is good news if you've got blue eyes and think your life is miserable at the moment. Blue is the color of truth, and someone with blue eyes can be relied upon to keep promises.

Green eyes are incredibly rare in China, but have occurred in a tiny handful of cases. To the ancient Chinese, they were a symbol of magical powers and secret knowledge because they were the same color as jade. Like jade, someone with green eyes is likely to be very honorable, because this precious stone can be broken, but never twisted. Jade protects the owner from evil spirits, so a person with green eyes is thought to have a special hotline to the spirit world. Such people will have a powerful sense of intuition, and often have friends in very high places.

Brown eyes are very common in China. They are a sign of steadfastness and reliability. Like the Earth element they represent, they are a symbol of great strength and powerful energy, but also of a very down-to-earth approach to life. People with brown eyes are easily bored by show-offs. They prefer the simple things in life and don't see why people should waste money on luxuries and designer goods. Never try to sell gold-plated chopsticks to someone with brown eyes, they will simply laugh at you.

Some people have *grey eyes*, or eyes that seem to switch between colors. They will flip from grey to light blue or light green, and then back again. But in Chinese face reading these changeable hues are simply listed as *grey*. Sometimes likened to the grey, changeable sea, grey-eyed people eyes are subject to great swings in temperament. One moment they can be calm and placid, and the next moment they might be raging in a massive storm. Grey eyes are a symbol of unpredictability. You can never be sure what a grey-eyed person is thinking, or what they will do next. They are as unpredictable to themselves as they are to others. They can never make up their minds; they are eternally ebbing to and fro like the tides of the sea.

Hazel eyes, which are a kind of greeny-brown, symbolize another kind of changeability. If you have hazel eyes, you may find other people keep on getting your color wrong because they look greener when you wear green and browner when you wear brown. This makes hazel eyes a symbol of a chameleon's ability to blend in, whatever the situation. People with hazel eyes need to be at the center of all the action, and gossip, and their shifting eye color helps to keep them camouflaged.

Almost unknown in the West, let alone China, are *Violet eyes*. This incredibly rare eye color is a sign of passion and deep emotion, great creativity and power over others. If you have violet eyes you are truly rare, like a tiger with wings, but your good fortune can work against you. It may be hard to make friends because nobody understands you, and people may fear you because you are so different.

People with *black eyes* have a slightly better fortune. If their brown eyes are so dark you can hardly see where the iris (the colored bit) meets the pupil (the black dot in the middle), then they will have a special characteristic. Just as their eyes are deep and unfathomable, so are they. Black eyes are difficult to read and people who have them can always keep secrets. But, they need to take care not to abuse this power or they run the risk of becoming professional liars.

Finally, if someone has *sparkly eyes* that seem to flash when they look your way, this is a sign of powerful energy bubbling away inside. Such people have so much energy zipping around their bodies that it shows up as a twinkle in their eyes. You can expect them to be bouncy and overactive, and possibly difficult to keep up with. They will always be one step ahead of everyone else. But, because they are always looking for new challenges, their enthusiasm may tire other people who are desperate to just put their feet up and rest.

Wait for It

But it doesn't stop there. There's more to the eye than the little bit with the color in it. The *white* of the eye is just as important as the colored area. Since most Chinese people's eyes are brown, we in the West need a different set of readings to get a better idea of someone's personality.

If the whites of your eyes are just that, white, it is a sign of energy and resourcefulness. White is the color of *bouncy energy* (known as Yang in Chinese), so very bright whites indicate a person who likes to be kept busy.

Some people have whites with a slightly bluish tinge to them. This is another sign of magical powers and intuition. Such people are likely to be very good at guessing games, and need very little information before they can solve problems and make decisions.

If the whites of the eyes have little red lines in them it means the veins are showing through the eyeball, and this is likely to be a sign of hard work or overindulgence. If you can see lots of spidery veins in your eyeball, try getting more rest and not staying up so late, otherwise you may find yourself yawning all during the day and having trouble concentrating.

If the whites are more yellow in color, it is a sign of *low energy* (known in Chinese as Yin). Yellowish eyes can be the result of a prolonged illness or a bad diet, and are likely to go hand-in-hand with low vitality and tiredness.

Amount of White

If there is a lot of white beneath the iris but very little or none above it, the person will seem from a distance to be permanently looking up. To the Chinese, this looks like an angry bull lowering his head before he charges, and is considered to be a sign of a hot temper. It is best to stay on the good side of someone with such eyes, and not to wave any red blankets around near them.

On the other hand, if there is a lot of white above the iris but none below, it gives a person the appearance of looking permanently down their nose at the world. This is a sign of a haughty attitude, and also indicates a person who is quick to judge and hard to please. In a person with eyes like these, even if he or she appears to be friendly, niceness will more likely be a sign of being well-brought up. Such people may be polite to you, but they are difficult to keep happy because they have very high standards. Still, if they do become your friends, you'll know it's because they are really impressed – and they're not impressed by much.

Some people have eyes that show large amounts of white all around, both above and below the iris, as well as in the usual left and right bits. This gives them the appearance of wide-eyed surprize, and they may find themselves always hearing shocking news. These people often have trouble with their health. They are no sooner recovered from one ailment, than they have another one to worry about. They may spend a lot of time complaining, but try not to hold it against them; they really do have more worries than most other people.

Lashes and Lids

Check the eyelashes as well. Long, soft lashes are a sign of gentleness and kindness. Someone who has these will be friendly to others and always want to live a peaceful life. If the lashes are short and stubby, it can be a sign of the opposite – a quick-tempered, active, perhaps violent person. Do your best not to get them angry.

Look out too for the eyelids. If someone has big, blinky upper lids like a cow or a sloth, they are likely to be a little slow off the mark. This isn't because they are stupid, but because they are often already quite happy with the way things are and don't see much point in changing them. If you need to convince them that something needs to be done fast, don't hold out too much hope. You will need to give a lot of very good reasons before you'll get them moving. "Look out, the house is on fire!" might be the only one that works.

If the lower eyelids seem bigger than those above the eye, it makes a person look like a lizard. Expect such people to be sly and cunning, and watch out that they don't try to trick you with one of their ruses. Be wary too of what they have to say. When a crocodile weeps, it could be pretending. Trust these people only if you are sure you really are their friend. If you're not, they won't think twice about feeding you to the alligators.

Face Value

- ☺ Remember **S**ome **P**eople **C**an **F**ly means check **S**hape, **P**osition, **C**olor, **F**eatures. It will stop you missing out important parts of a face reading.
- ☺ There's more to eyes than color alone. Check the angle, size, lashes, and lids, and don't forget the whites.

Face Facts: Eyes

EYE FEATURE	CHARACTERISTIC
Almond-shaped	Possibly vain
Almond-shaped and slanting up	Shrewd
Almond-shaped and slanting down	Confused, gullible
Very large	Childlike, gullible
Round and large	Artistic, outgoing
Small	Shy, intense, complacent, secretive
Deep-set	Intellectual, slow-starter
Sticky-out	Chancer, schmoozer
Eyes are close together	Stingy
Eyes are far apart	Charitable
Blue	Happy, bright
Green/Olive	Magical, intelligent
Brown	Strong, energetic
Grey/Changeable	Fickle, unpredictable
Hazel	Chameleon, likes to be involved
Violet	Charming, emotional
Black	Secretive
Sparkly	Overactive
Whites are very white	Powerful, energetic
Whites have bluish tint	Intuitive, magical
Whites are veiny	Overindulgence
Whites are yellowy	Low vitality

White shows beneath iris	Easily angered
White shows above iris	Snooty, hard to please
White shows all round	Possible ill health
Long lashes	Gentle, kind-hearted
Short lashes	Strong, aggressive
Heavy eyelids	Slow, complacent
Large lower lids	Sly, cunning

Face to Face

There's a picture of a movie star on your friend's wall. Something about the actress makes you uneasy. Her skin is a lovely, blushing pink, she has delicate, thin eyebrows and cute little double lines between her brows when she frowns. Her eyes are gorgeous: grey and slanting elegantly up in a classic Phoenix shape. But when you look closer at the picture, you see a tell-tale whiter area of skin between the brows. She has plucked hairs from there to make herself look prettier. What kind of person is she?

CHAPTER 6

Nosing Around

"This actress," I said. "She's hiding something."

"Very good," said Aunty Feng. "Go on."

"Delicate brows and Phoenix eyes mean she's beautiful, but she knows it and she expects everyone to do what she wants, like a spoiled child. Trouble is, she has grey eyes which means she doesn't really know what she wants and will keep changing her mind. So she's never pleased with anything. She's got a really fierce temper, too, what with the red skin, the double brow-lines and the joined brow that she's tried to hide. She might be pretty, but she's hell to please."

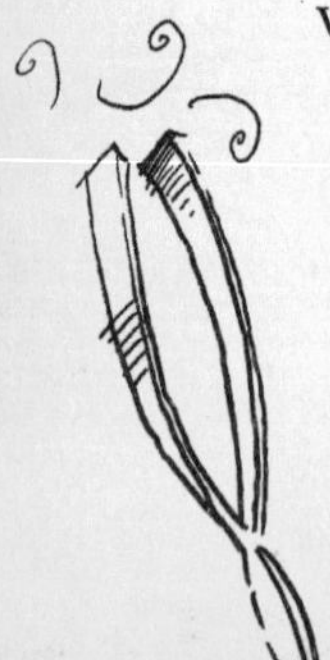

"Excellent," said Aunty Feng.

"But what about the plucked eyebrows?" I said. "Surely that changes her reading?"

"No," said Aunty Feng. "Wearing glasses doesn't make you smart, does it? You can wear a wig, get false teeth, or walk around on stilts all day, but it's not going to make any difference to the person you are inside. It might change the way other people look at you, but the real you is still underneath. Sometimes people want to hide that, which is why the face reader sometimes has to be a detective. But the face is a reflection of the fate, not the other way round."

"So, a nose job?"

"Won't change a thing. In fact, if you use a nose job to hide part of your character, Chinese sorcery says the nose will slowly grow back the way it was before. Which in your case would be a good thing."

"Would it?" I asked.

"Oh yes. You have such a sweet nose. You look like a little pig, with those big nose holes staring me in the face, and that cute little up-turned bit."

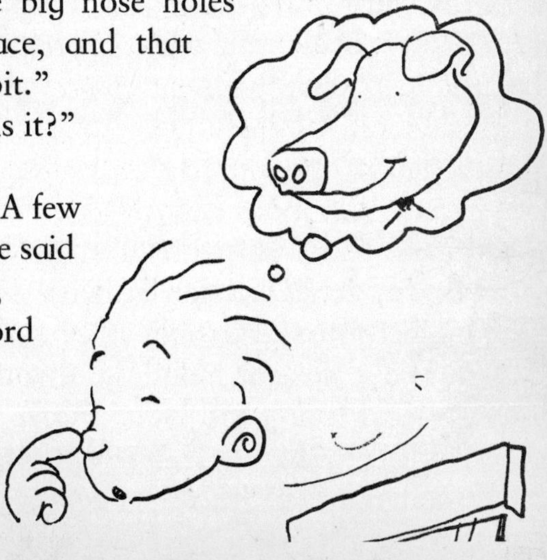

"And that's good, is it?" I asked.

"Nope," she said. "A few years ago I would have said that you were gullible, but I can't use that word now because it's been taken out of the dictionary."

"Has it?"

"Of course it

hasn't! Stupid boy!"

I felt my ears going very red.

"So, my nose tells you I'll fall for anything?"

"Yep, you'll be as much use in business as a fish on a bike."

"Er... Aunty Feng?"

"Yes, dear?"

"Why do fish need bikes?"

Nosing Around

The nose is one of the most important features on the face, because it actually connects you to the outside world. Your eyebrows just move around on top of your head, your eyes and ears provide you with information about the world around you, but your nose and mouth let in air and nourishment. A lot of the energy that goes into making up your soul is brought to you through your nose (as air) or mouth (as food and drink). This makes these two features crucial. They are also unique in that you only have one of each. People can live without one of their eyes or ears, because they would still be able to see or hear, but without your nose or mouth you wouldn't be able to smell or taste, and eating and breathing might be ever-so-slightly more difficult.

We sometimes use the term *nosy* to mean somebody who interferes with other people's private business. But to the

Chinese, a large nose is a sign of leadership, because it sticks out in front, like a general at the head of the army. The Chinese call an inventor, a founding father, or a great thinker a *nose-ancestor,* because they go forging ahead into new territory while everybody else is sitting around waiting for something to happen.

Nose Shape

A person's nose will give you plenty of information about how they behave with money, and how they are likely to do in business. If the nose is normal, it means the owner of it will be similarly unremarkable in money matters. They won't be rich, but they won't be poor either. Remember that it doesn't matter if you get a reading of *nothing special.* There will be plenty of other parts of the face to help you tell somebody's fortune.

Crooked Crooks

A straight nose is a sign of a reliable person with a basic good fortune – someone you can trust. But, not all noses are straight, some are crooked. In olden China it was thought that all noses were naturally straight, and that the only way you could get a crooked nose was if somebody smacked you in the face. Starting fights is not a very harmonious thing to do, so the Chinese are naturally suspicious of anyone who looks as if they have a history of getting into trouble. It's a little like inviting a man with an eye patch and a wooden leg to go sailing with you. He might not be a pirate, but do you really want to take the risk?

A crooked nose is a danger sign. It might mean the person is unreliable and gets into fights. Or, it might simply mean that they're unlucky, and have an unfortunate habit of walking into a lot of doors, tripping over steps, and jumping out of planes without a parachute. Whatever the reason behind their battered nose-shape, it's a good idea to think twice before involving yourself with such a person.

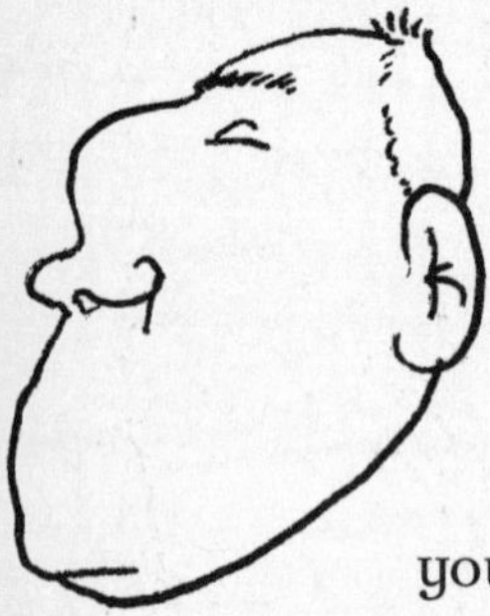

Ups and Downs

If the end of the nose turns downwards so that the nostrils are partly hidden and it looks a little like the beak of a hawk, this is a sign of a shrewd and canny individual. Like the hawk itself, this person has a mind that soars above the everyday world, and swoops down on its target at exactly the right moment. The down-turned nose is a sign of a business genius. But the hawk is a bird of prey, and just because it's good at what it does, that doesn't make it an ideal friend, especially if you're a little mouse or a cute fluffy bunny. Hawk-nosed people are clever and successful traders, but check the rest of their face fortune to see if they will also be loyal, honest friends.

If the nose turns up at the end, displaying the nostrils, and looking like a ski-jump from the side, it resembles a pig's snout and is a sign of an innocent, gullible business sense. Anyone with a piggy nose is a walking disaster in the business world because they can't keep secrets, sometimes open their mouth without putting their brain in gear, and are easily swindled. Pigs don't have wings like the smart hawk, they have to oink across the muddy ground and take the long way round. And if somebody's looking for a bacon sandwich, the pig is easy pickings. If you have a piggy nose, count to ten before you make any important decisions, and try not to give in to persistent sales people. If you're going shopping for something important or expensive, try to take one of your less gullible friends with you, otherwise you may find yourself being taken for a ride.

Nose Color

Whatever your basic skin color, your blood flows close to the surface of your nose, so it should be ever-so-slightly pinker than the rest of you.

If your nose is paler than the rest of your face, possibly looking white or greyish, then the blood in your body doesn't have time to hang around in the middle of your face. It's all off somewhere else, fighting an internal fire, defusing a bomb, or holding off bandit germs. In other words, your nose is pale because your body is trying to fight off an infection. A pale nose is a sure sign that you should get some rest or something decent to eat. If you see somebody else with a pale nose, you can almost guarantee that they are, or soon will be, feeling a little under the weather.

If the nose is much redder than the rest of the face, looking a little like that of a clown, it's a sign that someone's blood is too lazy to get up and move around away from the center of their face. It's a sign that the owner of the red nose has been indulging in too much food or drink, and could do with some healthy living for a while. Tell them they shouldn't have so many late nights and watch as they bluster and fret, trying to pretend you're wrong.

If the nose is slightly purple in color, or darker than the rest of the face without being red, this is a sign of somebody working hard in secret. Whatever they're doing during the day, they're also likely to be sneaking off to moonlight on another job, or go to classes to learn some new skill. A purplish nose is a good indicator that the owner is destined for promotion. They are definitely up to something, and chances are high indeed that it will benefit them in the future.

Highs and Lows

A high bridge to the nose is another sign of good fortune in money matters. The higher up the face the nose starts, the more lucky breaks the owner can expect. A high nose is a sign of success without effort. The owner might never be satisfied and continue to work hard without ever noticing how lucky they were to start with. If you know someone who works in a supermarket for extra money, even though their parents own three banks and twelve yachts, the chances are quite high that you're looking at a typical high-nose type. He genuinely works for the money, but doesn't notice that none of the other kids get dropped off at school by their dad's helicopter. But this is a good sign. At least he understands that money doesn't grow on trees, and wants to earn his own. High-nose types will make excellent sales people, because they're prepared to make the effort to knock on doors and tout for business, and their natural good luck will take care of the rest.

On the other hand, a nose with a low bridge that starts low down the face is a sign that the owner may have to struggle in money matters. The lower the nose, the less the owner will realize just how much they're missing. If you know anyone who complains all the time about not having

any money, but who won't lift a finger to do any work, you're probably looking at a low-nose type. Such people will sit in front of a television that doesn't work properly, wrapped up in blankets because they can't afford to turn on the heating, waiting for someone else to wash the dishes and cook the dinner. This is because a low bridge isn't just a sign of bad fortune in money matters, it also suggests that the owner won't notice what they're missing out on.

Fats and Thins

A thin, delicate nose in olden China was a sign of beauty, in both women and men, but it also suggests selfishness. With such a lovely nose, the reasoning goes, people would be used to getting their own way, and so would probably become very vain, spoiled, or overly critical of others. After all, if you know you're gorgeous, it's sometimes all too easy to tell everybody else how much nicer they would look if only they had a prettier nose.

A broad nose, however, is a sign of a dependable person who is kind to others. Broad foundations for the nose are thought to be the same as broad foundations for life. A wide nose is usually a sign of a person with a wide range of interests, great patience, and an easy manner that avoids criticizing other people's failings.

Tip Top Tips

The tip of the nose is the easiest guide to someone's luck with money. Think of it as a sack of money, the larger it is, the more money the owner will have during their life. A big, bulbous nose means incredible wealth, a tiny pointed one means very little money.

But, since this is Chinese face reading, it isn't quite as simple as that. It's still possible for someone with a huge clown-size nose to be poorer than a friend with a pointy nose, because we don't stop examining the nose at the tip. While the tip of the nose tells us how much money somebody will have, it's the nostrils that tell us how much they will actually spend.

The nostrils, holes in the face, will tell you the size of the holes in the owner's pockets. The bigger the nostrils, the more money they will throw around, whether they've got it or not. So, someone whose nose is fat and broad with gigantic cavernous nostrils will be a real big-spender. They'll have a fat wallet and a huge desire to paint the town red. They'll always have money to spare, and they can't resist treating themselves to simply everything that takes their fancy. "Oh, come on!" they'll shout when you ask if they *really* need a musical toilet, "Money's no use if you can't spend it and enjoy it!"

If someone has a small, thin nose-tip and tiny nostrils, it means they don't spend much money, which is a bit of luck because they'll never have much to spend. This nose type will always give you a wise word about making and saving money. They'll tell you that having one penny more than you need makes you rich, and being a penny short makes you poor.

But what happens if the set-up isn't quite so neat? What if someone has a little nose with big nostrils? In that case, they'll be very poor, because they'll spend, spend, spend, even when they're broke, broke, broke. They'll never have enough money because they'll always spend more than they have.

If someone has a huge, broad nose-tip but tiny little nostrils, they'll have loads of money, but they won't ever want to spend any of it. They risk turning into misers, counting their money all day, but never doing anything exciting, adventurous, or wacky with it. These people really annoy bank clerks because they have a habit of withdrawing all their cash just so they can look at it, and then putting it back again. People in banks really hate that. It wastes their time or, in other words, really puts their noses out of joint.

Face Value

☺ Always look beyond the obvious. People can change the

way they look, but it won't change the way they are. Check for tell-tale signs of cosmetic alteration.

☺ The nose is all about money and business sense. The bigger, the better.

☺ The nostrils are all about spending. The bigger the nostrils, the bigger the holes in your pockets.

Face Facts: Nose

NOSE FEATURE	READING
Straight nose	Fortunate, reliable
Crooked nose	Unlucky, unreliable
Down-turned nose	Shrewd, careful, smart
Up-turned nose	Tactless, boastful, simple
Thin nose	Vain, critical
Broad nose	Unassuming, moderate
Slightly pink nose	Wealth and good fortune
Red nose	Overindulgence
White/greyish nose	Potential illness
Greenish nose	Confusion, imprisonment
Purply/dark nose	Promotion
High bridge	Fortune and ease of living
Low bridge	Adversity, lack of energy
Large tip	Great wealth
Small tip	Low income
Wide, flaring nostrils	Extrovert, generous
Thin, pinched nostrils	Introvert, miserly
Really, really wide flaring nostrils	Extravagant (even if poor)
Really, really small nostrils	Miserly (even if rich)

Face to Face

Your friend wants to borrow money from you. His nose turns downwards and he has small nostrils. His eyes are big and blue, his ears are large, and he has straight no-nonsense eyebrows. If you lend him the money, will you ever see it again?

CHAPTER 7

Mouthing Off

"Got the answer, yet?" asked Aunty Feng.

"It's a toughie," I said. "You've deliberately tried to confuse me."

"But?"

"But, this is a great person to lend money to. His eyes say he's got a good heart and won't lie to you, and his ears say he has good fortune. Normally, that wouldn't be important, but here it's about what he *does* with the money. He has a nose for business, and small nostrils hidden underneath a down-turned tip. This means he wouldn't ask for that money unless he really needed it. But he's wise with cash, so whatever he intends to do with it will repay him tenfold. If you're a good enough friend to lend him the money, he'll give it back with interest."

"Yes," said Aunty Feng. "Well done. The nose alone

suggests you might get swindled by a canny businessman, but you used the other parts of the face to see that you were dealing with a kind, honest person. Well done."

"It was nothing," I said.

"I suppose you're right," she said, thoughtfully. "Anyone could have worked that out in time. You're not that smart after all."

Me and my big mouth.

Loud and Proud

A big mouth suggests the owner of it is a really big talker, and that can mean a lot of things. They enjoy talking to everyone they meet which might mean they're friendly, good at getting on with other people, and are rarely shy or afraid. But they might enjoy talking to annoy other people, and endlessly complain about tiny problems, or mistakes that may or may not have really happened. You can spot this kind of person by comparing the mouth and the brows. Are they scowling all the time? If they are, you can guess what they'll use their big mouth for.

A third possibility is that if someone has a big mouth and little ears, it probably means they listen to themselves but not to others. They like talking purely to hear the sound of their own voice, and this makes them awful bores.

Remember, any of these could apply, so you'll need to do some serious thinking. That's why we save the mouth till last when reading the major aspects of a face. By the time you get to the mouth, you'll already have a pretty good idea of the person's character, and this will give you some clues about to how to interpret it.

A big mouth also suggests loudness, and not just volume either. Someone with a big-mouth will probably like bright, flashy clothes, and enjoy clowning around and showing off. A big mouth is a useful asset if you want to tell the world something you think is important, either about yourself or about other people. For this reason, big-mouths make excellent journalists or comedians.

Small is Beautiful

There are just as many different readings from a small mouth. Maybe people with small mouths don't need to talk much, and prefer their own company. They might be shy, or perhaps they just don't get the chance to put their views across. While the big-mouths are yelling at each other and throwing things, the small-mouthed person is politely putting up their hand and waiting to be heard. But sometimes they can be so meek, nobody notices they have something to say.

The mouth may be tiny because the owner doesn't like

talking to others. They might be shy, or they might be anti-social and snobbish, preferring to avoid human company, not because they are meek, but because they think other people are stupid.

People with small mouths are likely to hold grudges, mainly because they don't complain when they should. If someone with a small mouth finds a fly in their soup, they won't tell the waiter. Instead, they'll just mutter about it to themselves and have a thoroughly miserable time. While the big-mouth complains loudly, annoying the manager and no doubt getting a free meal and loads of bribes to shut them up, the small-mouth just looks at the soup and vows to sneak back in when everyone's gone home and dynamite the kitchens.

Because they're good at keeping secrets and can have a mean streak in their characters, people with small mouths make great spies. People with big mouths might pretend to be secret agents to impress their friends, but it's the quiet person at the back pretending to read the paper who's the real thing.

Say, "Aaaah"

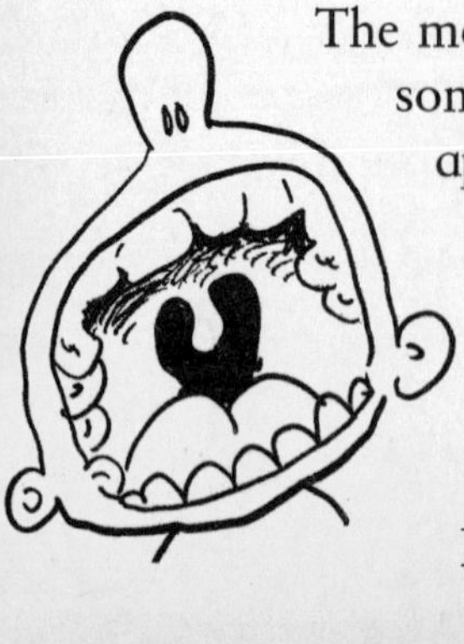

The mouth can also be used for determining somebody's energy levels. Energy, or *qi*, appears in the mouth as saliva, and the more *qi* somebody has, the wetter their mouth. If someone is permanently drooling, with big flubbery wet lips, they have a surfeit of *qi*, and are likely to be very emotional. Like a big, bouncy dog who doesn't know when to sit still, such a person will leap all over the place looking for fun, even when everyone else is trying to concentrate on something important. Just imagine a slobbering puppy licking your face when you're trying to read a book. It makes you feel icky just thinking about it. Well, that's often the effect that the over-energetic person has on others. Other people might get annoyed because they could do without interference just now, thank you very much. If you see someone with a slobbery wet mouth, you'll know that you need to be firm with them, otherwise they'll be dragging you out to the park to throw sticks and jump in puddles. Maybe you'd like that!

If someone's mouth is dry and parched, their energy levels are quite low. There isn't enough *qi* to keep the mouth wet. This person may be slow and lethargic. The slobbery, wet-mouthed person will be running round the room, chasing their tail and trying to get everybody to go outside and play catch, but dry-mouthed people will sit on the sofa, saying they're too tired. "Never do today what you can put off till tomorrow," is the motto of dry-mouthed couch potatoes, but they'll never admit it. It's not because they're lazy, it's just that the dryness of the mouth makes them reluctant to do anything too strenuous. For them, it's as if they've just crawled across a hot desert for two weeks under the burning sun. When they finally reach the beautiful cool shade of an oasis, the last thing they

need is to go bungee jumping. They just want to put their feet up and have a rest.

Straight Talking

The shape of the mouth is determined by the position and thickness of the lips. Most people have straight, unassuming lips of medium width. Because the Chinese always like to look on the bright side, they assume that this perfectly normal mouth-shape means the owner will have good fortune.

If the mouth is straight but the lips are thick and bold, this is known as the *Cow mouth*. The Cow mouth suggests that the owner has a long, happy life to look forward to because they will have something to offer the world. Cows give milk, and so live far longer on a farm than any other kind of animal. Long after the pig has been turned into bacon and the chicken has been dipped in barbecue sauce, the cow is still happily munching away in her field. So if you have a Cow mouth, it means you'll be around long after all the other animals have gone to market.

A straight mouth with thinner lips is even more fortunate, because it looks like no beast known on Earth. The Chinese think that the only creature with this kind of mouth was the dragon, and because the dragon stands for power and the Emperor, the owner of a *Dragon mouth* will have a powerful career in later life.

Smiley Faces

What if your lips are of average thickness, but your mouth turns up at the corners? It looks as if you're smiling all the time, which means that you'll always have something to be happy about.

If your lips are thick and you still have that sneaky smile on your face, you have what the Chinese call a *Moon mouth*. This is because if you turn your head on its side, your mouth will look like a crescent moon. The Moon mouth is the sign of a real party animal, someone who's always out enjoying themselves, no matter what the occasion. Once again, it's a sign that you'll always be happy, but you should remember that there's more to life than having fun. Also, there are some occasions when other people may not take kindly to your infectious merry-making. Try not to get the fancy dress party mixed up with the funeral, or you may end up causing trouble.

If the mouth turns upwards but the lips are thinner than usual, this gives the owner a *Goat mouth*. Like these tough, nimble mountain creatures, the owner of a Goat mouth will always manage to eke out a living in difficult circumstances. The goat can eat all sorts of disgusting foods and climb the most hazardous mountain paths in its search for new pastures, but this ability has two sides. The owner of a Goat mouth might be able to survive in horrible

circumstances, but quite often they don't have to. Nobody makes the goats go up into the cold mountain peaks, and nobody makes them climb steep rock-falls in search of a bit of chewy moss. Why don't they just stay down in the pastures like the sensible cows?

What about the old fairy tale in which a trio of goats try to cross a bridge guarded by a hungry troll? Didn't any of them think of crossing by a different route? Of course not, because goats can be stubborn creatures when they feel like it. The owner of a Goat mouth is liable to be proud of living through hardship, but should always look around to see if there isn't an easier way. They may be so busy congratulating themselves on what they're achieving, they don't notice there's a much better route staring them in the face.

Moping Around

Some people have mouths that curve downwards which makes them look permanently miserable. This doesn't mean they will have bad luck. It is possible they will have plenty of money, a successful life, and a loving family. But even if they do, someone with a down-turned mouth may still feel miserable. They are fated never to count their blessings. No matter how well things are going in life, no matter how lucky they may be, compared with less fortunate people all around the world, a person with a down-

turned mouth will still mope and moan and fret. This is a sign of the eternal worrier, and of someone who always has something, however small, to complain about.

If the lips are thick on a down-turned mouth, making the owner look like a sour old toad, this person really will have something to groan about. Where the person with a sad-looking normal mouth might just complain every now and then, the person with thick lips and a down-turned mouth can probably think of ten disastrous things that happened to them before breakfast, and they won't be making it up either. This person will be surrounded by hardships for their entire life. They run the eternal risk of being hit by falling satellites, locking themselves out of their house, or winning the lottery but losing the ticket, possibly all at the same time. Their best bet is to make sure they hang around with friends who have better face fortunes. At least then they'll know nothing too terrible will happen. But even so, they could be walking between two lucky friends and still be the only one to fall down an open man-hole.

If someone has a down-turned mouth but thin lips, they'll look more like a witless little frog. This pinched, thin grimace can be seen on people's faces when they're trying to smile their troubles away. It's a sign that whatever their problems may be, they'll always be hopeful. "Try to look on the bright side," the frog-faced mother will say when dad's car gets squashed by a steam-roller. "At least we don't have to worry about those squeaking brakes, anymore." In a way, the *Frog mouth* is better than the Toad mouth, because at least the owner has a positive attitude, but sometimes even the brightest and sunniest of people need to admit that things just aren't going right. The Frog-mouthed person will dust themselves off and keep on going, when a lot of more sensible people would give up and find something else to do.

Lippy

When the face is turned sideways, does one lip stick out further than the other? If it does, then we have an extra face reading.

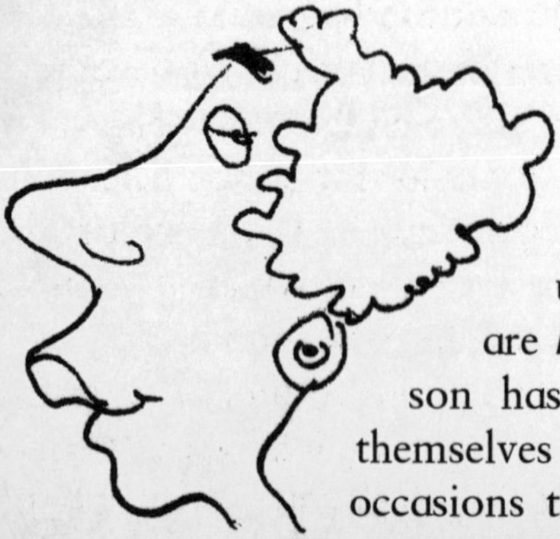

If the top lip sticks out in front of the bottom lip, the owner has a habit of keeping quiet even when they should be speaking up. This is because their lips are *buttoned* together. This person has a lot of trouble making themselves heard, because on the rare occasions they do want to say something, they're too timid to raise their voices. This makes them appear shy and hesitant, especially when it comes to speaking.

If the bottom lip sticks out in front of the top lip, the owner looks like a pouting, angry child, and if they don't get exactly what they want, when they want it, they'll simply sulk. Such people are very selfish and difficult to deal with. Not only are they used to getting their own way, they also think that sulking is the only way to get things done.

Color of Mouth

The mouth is also useful for determining the state of somebody's health. After all, it's not for nothing that the doctor asks you to stick your tongue out and say, "Ahh." It's easy to get an idea of someone's condition by checking the color of their mouth. The same applies to everybody because no matter what color our skin is, we're all the same color on the inside. There is only one correct color for a mouth, and that is a healthy, pinkish red. If your mouth is this color, then you have the standard Chinese reading, which you should know by heart by now: good fortune and good health.

Some people have a mouth or tongue that is greyish or white in hue. This is a bad sign and indicates that they are ill. Even if they protest that they feel absolutely fine, you should pack them off to a doctor at once, because they are probably just about to come down with a hideous disease. A white or greyish mouth is also taken by the Chinese to be a sign of general bad fortune because if you're sick you aren't able to do any of the things that could improve your life. You can't work, play, go out, or study, so illness freezes your fortune at the point you got sick. Wrap up warm, get some rest, and try not to worry so much.

Dents

But that's not all there is to the mouth. There's even a Chinese fortune attached to the little dent in the middle of the top lip. This rules the various ages and stages we go through as we grow up.

The longer the dent, the longer you can expect to live. The average dent is about the same length as the top part of your little finger, perhaps a little bit shorter. If the distance between your nose and mouth is longer than that, you stand a very good chance of living to be quite ancient.

The ideal dent is formed by two little parallel lines, one below each nostril. If the lines are slanting instead of vertical, the direction of the slope is a warning of hardship. If the dent slants towards your lip in a kind of \/ shape, you can expect some hard times in your later years. You'll need to examine the rest of your face fortune to determine what problems will beset you, but a \/ dent is a sure-fire sign of something going wrong when you're quite old. The best thing to hope for is that it's something minor, like your car not starting on your 70th birthday or your favorite trousers going out of fashion just before your 80th disco. The best way to ensure that it doesn't make too much difference is to make sure you don't take too many risks. Once you're old and grey, remember your face fortune and try to avoid anything that looks like a disaster waiting to happen. Don't bet your family fortune on a horse, don't play chicken with giant trucks when you're on roller-skates, and don't go trampolining with your grandchildren. It's too risky, your face fortune says so. And don't say I didn't warn you.

The alternative is to have a dent that slants towards the nose in a kind of /\ shape. This indicates high chances of hardship in one's youth, but since you're not a baby, this may mean that the difficult times have already been and gone. If you were involved in a nasty accident when you were a child, or were the kind of toddler who was always bumping into things, then the dent in your top lip will give the fact away to anyone who can read faces. That's the bad news. The good news is that your

troubles are far behind you, so when you're an old codger you can happily roller-skate under a truck on your way to a trampolining contest where you've bet a horse that it can't play chicken with your grandchildren. Or something.

And Teeth

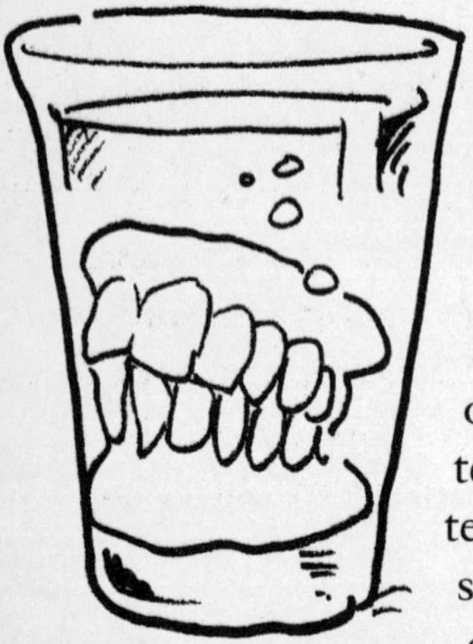

Teeth were vitally important in ancient China. Without them you had no choice but to live on soup and soft noodles. The more teeth you had, the luckier you were. In a world without dentists most people stood to lose their teeth as they got older. The Chinese didn't have false teeth either, so if all the emperor's teeth fell out he had to get one of his servants to chew his food for him and spit it into his mouth.

As far as the Chinese are concerned, the more teeth you have, the luckier you are. This belief may have had something to do with the growth of the wisdom teeth, which turn up in the back of your mouth in your late teens or early twenties. The problem with wisdom teeth is that some people don't have enough space in their jaw to fit them in. They sometimes grow crooked and have to be pulled out. If you have thirty-two or more teeth in your head, your face fortune is very lucky indeed. Having that many in your mouth was incredibly rare in olden days, because you were almost guaranteed to lose some through hard knocks, bad health, or plain bad luck.

Beware of the Fairies

Teeth don't become part of your face fortune until you get the second set. There's not much difference between one person's baby teeth and another's, and we all know they're destined to fall out quite quickly. Because baby teeth are there for such a short time, they are not very useful for guessing somebody's fortune.

The Tooth Fairy was never as important to the ancient Chinese as it is to us. If a sorcerer wanted to put a curse on somebody he would need something that belonged to them, and the more important the possession, the stronger the spell would become. This is why the people of old were very protective about their hair and nail clippings, but teeth are much longer-lasting, and actually grow out of the jawbone, making them one of the most powerful objects of all.

Grin to Win

The whiter the teeth, the luckier you are, and this has less to do with Chinese face reading than common sense. If you have white teeth it means you've looked after them, and that will always decrease the chances of cavities, tooth decay, and gum disease.

If you have big teeth, and can manage a really broad grin, your fortune promises a long life, but one that will involve a lot of hard work. If your teeth are quite small, you'll show more gum when you smile, and this could mean selfishness. Somebody with tiny little teeth will look more like a small child, and very young children are usually too interested in themselves to care much about others.

The two upper front teeth are also important. The one

on the right shows how well you get on with your family, and the one on the left shows how you get on with your friends. If they are firm and even, then you're in luck, but if one of them is crooked there will be difficulties with the group it represents. If one is knocked out then you can expect serious trouble.

Tooth and Claw

If somebody has long, pointed incisors, a bit like a vampire or a wolf, they are cunning individuals and very hard to fool. But they are also fiercely defensive, and likely to hold a grudge for a long time.

If somebody has flat, chunky teeth like a cow, they are passive and carefree, happy to sit around in their field all day, chewing the grass and occasionally farting or going "moo". They are quite gullible people but, beware, they are just as easy as wolves to excite to anger, and are just as likely to charge. Remember what happens when you wave a red rag at a bull? The good thing, however, is that people with Cow teeth are easier to please, and willing to forgive.

Some people have teeth that slant inwards, like those of a shark. Shark's teeth are in that position because it allows them to bite and hold on. In fact, it also means they have trouble letting go even when they want to. The same applies for people with Shark teeth; they can be very possessive and hard to shake off. Many of them are fated, like the shark itself, to be very solitary animals, prowling on their own, either not wanting or not keeping friends.

But you can also have teeth that slant forwards, sticking out at the front like those of a goat. Goat's teeth stick outwards so that they can chomp at the grass closer to the ground, which means they get a better meal for less work. This is very important on the sparse, rocky mountainside, and Goat teeth signify that their owner is also suitably shrewd and smart. They also suggest that, unlike the lonesome shark, the owner of the Goat teeth likes to be part of the crowd, roaming with the herd and generally getting on well with other people.

Face Value

☺ The reading for a part of a face can sometimes change depending on what the rest of the features tell us. Don't immediately make a decision on the basis of one feature. Check the others too and see if they give you a new perspective.

Face Facts: Mouths

MOUTH FEATURE	READING
Big mouth	Extrovert/show-off
Little mouth	Introvert/meek
Slobbery	Emotional, energetic
Dry	Lack of *qi*, lethargic
Straight/normal lips	Good fortune
Straight/thick lips (Cow)	Long life
Straight/thin lips (Dragon)	Powerful career
Up-turned/normal lips	Happiness
Up-turned/thick lips (Tiger)	Party animal
Up-turned/thin lips (Goat)	Hardship
Down-turned/normal lips	Worry
Down-turned/thick lips (Toad)	Hardship
Down-turned/thin lips (Frog)	Always hopeful
Top lip sticks past bottom lip	Shy, unassertive
Bottom lip sticks past top lip	Petulant, selfish
Rosy red color	Good fortune
Grey/whitish	Illness
Long dent in top lip	Long life
Dent is V-shaped	Hardship in old age
Dent is Λ-shaped	Hardship in early years
Lots of teeth	Good fortune
Missing teeth	Accident-prone
White teeth	Lucky
Yellow teeth	Lethargic
Green teeth	Very ill

Broad grin/big teeth	Long life
Little teeth	Childish, selfish
Pointed, wolf teeth	Cunning
Flat teeth (Cow)	Complacent, gullible
Inward-pointing, Shark teeth	Lonely, solitary
Sticky-out, Goat teeth	Shrewd, energetic, gregarious

Face to Face

You need someone to babysit your dog while you're away on holiday, and a friend volunteers. He has a brownish tint to his skin, big ears, blue eyes that slant downwards, and sticky-out Goat teeth. He also has a gap in his eyebrow. Is he a good bet, or is he a walking disaster?

CHAPTER 8

Hair Flair

"You're taking a long time," said Aunty Feng.

"That's because I'm up to my neck in red herrings!" I said snappily.

"Why's that?"

"Most of the points on his face don't mean anything. Or rather, they mean something, but nothing that influences his talents as a dog-sitter."

"So, what have you come up with?"

"Well, brown skin says reliable, big ears say good fortune and a good heart, so that looks like someone who'd mean what he said when he promised to look after the dog. He's got blue eyes so he'll be happy for a lot of the time. And the Goat teeth say he'll always be dragging the dog out for walks because he's raring to go. But it's the other clues I don't understand. Downward slanting eyes mean he could be bitter, and the gappy eyebrow means he'll hold a grudge, but if he's volunteering for the job, I can't see what he has to get grouchy about."

"So?"

"So, I guess he'd be a good dog-sitter, but I should make sure he knows how much I appreciate it, otherwise he'll feel used. Then he'll sulk and won't ever help me out again."

"Sounds like a good reading to me," said Aunty Feng.

"But it's getting really complicated," I said. "Each new feature just adds more influences."

"But it doesn't make things more confusing," said Aunty Feng. "It just makes them more exact."

"I suppose so," I said. "I'm glad there aren't any more features left to learn."

"Are, too," said Aunty Feng.

"Are not!"

"Are, too!" she yelled, grabbing my hair.

"Ouch! What are you doing?" I yelled.

"I'm showing you another feature of the face," said Aunty Feng.

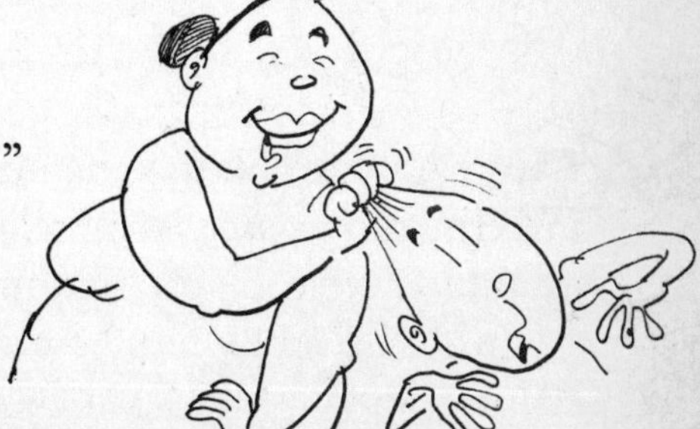

"It's not part of the face," I winced. "It's part of the head."

"Look," said Aunty Feng, "I don't make the rules, I just do the talking, OK?"

"All right, all right," I shouted, and she let go. "So, I

guess hair's pretty simple, just different colors and that's more or less it, right?"

"Some People Can Fly," said Aunty Feng in a warning voice. "Even hair has Shape, Position, Color, and Features."

"Features! What features are there in hair?"

"Aha!" said Aunty Feng with a flourish. "Well, for example, if someone's hair is thin—"

"Come on," I said. "Who wants fat hair?"

"Pay attention," she growled, smacking me with her fan.

Crowning Glory

Hair grows out of the face, and hence tells us a lot about the person underneath it. If it is badly kept, that is a sure sign that the person is too preoccupied with their troubles to look after themselves. The condition and color of hair is determined by the energy (or *qi*) of its owner. If you're tired, rushed off your feet, or preoccupied, your hair won't have the kind of bounce and sheen it ought to. Your hair is your crowning glory, so make sure you look after it. And the best way to look after your hair is to look after yourself.

The Long and the Short

During the Manchu dynasty, when China was ruled by foreign emperors, men were forced to shave part of their heads so that their hairline went right across the top of the

head from ear to ear. This was the old Manchu symbol of slavery, and the people stopped doing it as soon as they had the chance. But they would grow the bit at the back as long as possible, and wear it in a long braid. Long, unbraided, free-flowing hair on men has always been a sign of rebellion in China; even in recent times, some Chinese-speaking countries had customs officials waiting in airports with shears to make sure that no rebels came across the border. Cut a rebel's long hair, they believed, and you sap his strength. Rock stars beware.

Long hair on a girl is a sign of beauty and lack of worry. The longer and better-kept a girl's hair, the more spare time she has to spend fiddling with it, so the richer she must be. If it is really, really long, she must hardly have time to do anything else, and she might be a little vain. Pigtails on either side of the head are a sign of innocence, because it's a very childish hairstyle in China.

Very, very short hair on men means that someone is too busy to devote any thought to the way their head looks.

It is the sign of the military officer, but also of anyone who has no time for appearances because their mind is on other things. Many young boys in China have extremely short hair, or even shave their heads, so that they can save time washing and brushing and get on with studying instead. Short hair on a girl implies a business-like manner, or a woman who puts her career first.

Hair Color

In the Far East, strong, dark hair has always been thought best. The darker the hair, the more energy someone has to spare to make the color deeper. Light-colored hair, especially if it is dry or has split ends, means that someone is like a cactus in the desert, so deprived of energy that they are sucking up *qi* from the people around them. Blonds may have more fun, but everybody else has to put up with watching them and that can get on your nerves after a while. Brown hair, or *tea hair*, is a sign of someone who keeps up with the times. Fiery red hair is a symbol of magical powers and, predictably, of a short temper.

If your hair is drab and mousy, it means your *qi* is not strong enough to make up its mind, and neither are you. Grey hair is a sign of old age and wisdom, and demands respect. Even now in some parts of Asia there are special

grey seats on trains, reserved especially for old people. Grey hair in someone young is a sign that their *qi* has been sapped, perhaps by a vampire or more usually by overbearing parents. If someone has a bolt of grey hair like a skunk, or bolts of grey at the sides of their head, it is a sign that they have sacrificed part of their *qi* to gain special powers, and means you may be looking at a sorcerer.

Artificial Alterations

If hair is dyed, it might be harder for you to read a face, but it doesn't change the person underneath. Changing your hair color won't make you a better or worse person, it will just disguise some of the clues. Look at the roots of the hair to see the natural color coming through.

Wigs might make people with no hair look younger, but since many men in China shave their heads there's not much point in wearing a wig. Rather than waste time trying to make sure that a wig is straight or won't get blown off by the wind, Chinese men would rather go bald gracefully, especially since a bald head demands more respect.

As for hair extensions, that's cheating. Growing and caring for long hair takes time and effort, and someone who just throws money at a hairdresser to glue somebody else's hair onto their own is wasting their time if they want to impress anyone.

The Rough with the Smooth

Very fine hair shows that someone is sensitive and creative, possibly very shy. If the hair seems sparse, it's a sign of worry and stress, and of someone who may be getting old before their time because they work so hard. No hair at all, of course, means someone who has gone bald because of overwork and worry.

Drab hair that lies flat around the face is a sign of someone without much oomph in their life, who is happy to follow orders and reluctant to take the initiative. But hair that is straight and bouncy (like you've just walked out of a hair salon) is a sign of a good-hearted individual.

Coarse, tufty hair that's stiff, frizzy, or hard to manage is a sign of a person with a strong, forceful personality, possibly even stubborn and unwilling to change their mind.

Curly Wurly

Curly hair is a sign of resilience and smartness, because it pushes free of the head like tough weeds and brambles. Chinese people are not generally born with curly hair, and so believe that curls have to be artificial. If someone has too much curly hair, they are regarded as vain because they would have had to invest so much effort with rollers and tongs to get the effect. If you have naturally curly hair, your face fortune is one of being hot-headed and liable to fly off the handle at a moment's notice, especially if the curls look messy.

Beardy Weirdy

In China, a beard is a sign of wisdom, because you have to be a very old man before you stand any chance of growing one. A Chinese beard is normally a small, droopy moustache and a little spike of hair on the chin. More hair than that, and a sorcerer will know you're trying to hide something, so beware of barbarians with big bushy beards you could lose a hamster in. This belief is rooted in the olden days when some Chinese warriors grew large beards to hide any ugly battle scars they might have on their faces. The beard also changes the shape of a man's face. One of the classic joke-shop disguises is a beard and glasses, because they hide the most important lines in a face; a beard can cover the neck and chin and make it very difficult to remember how somebody used to look. Many prisoners in China used to let their beards grow out as far as possible, so that if they escaped they could shave in a trice, knowing that few of

the guards would be able to recognize them without all that hair on their faces.

As with many other parts of personal appearance, the important thing is neatness and evenness. If a man takes care of his beard, he can't really go wrong, although the Chinese do have one further thing to add about weird beards. If someone's beard requires an incredible amount of effort to maintain, such as a handlebar moustache, then that is a sign of vanity. Check as well for stubble behind the ears. If a man has it, then his skin has been stretched back during plastic surgery, which may have altered some of the other features on his face.

Face Value

- ☺ Hair shows your energy level, or *qi*.
- ☺ Glossy, healthy hair means healthy energy levels. Bad hair means a troubled spirit.
- ☺ Neat hair is good, but if your hair requires hours and hours of maintenance, you need to get a life.

Face Facts: Hair

HAIR FEATURE	READING
Dark hair	High *qi* levels, energetic
Light hair	Low *qi* levels, lethargic
Blonde hair	Fun-loving
Red hair	Magical, hot-tempered
Brown hair	Keeps up with the times
Grey hair	Distinguished, mature
Grey hair (when young)	Tired, hardworking
Mousy hair	Indecisive
Two-tone hair	Sorcerer
Long hair (males)	Rebellious
Very long hair (females)	Idleness (risk of vanity)
Short hair (females)	Efficient
Very short hair (males)	Military, bold
Fine hair	Creative, shy
Thin hair	Worried, stressed
No hair	Worried, stressed, venerable
Drab, flat hair	Unassertive
Bouncy hair	Lucky, easygoing
Curly hair	Tough, resilient
Very curly hair	Vain, self-regarding
Straight hair	Good heart
Wild hair	Wild person
Neat hair	Neat person
Coarse, frizzy hair	Forceful, stubborn
Beard or moustache	Wisdom
Bushy beard	Hiding something

Face to Face

There's been an accident on your camping trip. You're the only one with first-aid skills so you have to stay with the injured person, but one of your two friends must go across the fields in search of help. But it's quite a way to go. Friend (A) is a boy with wild, frizzy hair that looks as if he's just been pulled backwards through a hedge. Friend (B) has beautiful, long blond hair like a waterfall of pure gloss and fluffiness. She says her sister's a nurse. Which of them do you send on the long trek to get an ambulance?

CHAPTER 9

Spots and Dots

"There are three answers to that," I said. "One, the other, or both."

"But what's the correct answer?"

"Well, it's not her," I said. "So what if her sister's a nurse, you just said I was the only one with any first-aid skills, so she's obviously just showing off. That's the last thing we need. We want the stubborn, energetic kid with the frizzy hair who's going to keep marching until he hits a hospital. And if they don't believe him, he's mad enough to steal an ambulance and drive it over here himself."

"OK. But why not send them both?"

"Because she'll get halfway across the first field and start yelling, 'Urgh! Cowpats! How disgusting! I refuse to go another step without my four-wheel-drive!' A couple of minutes of that and the other kid will get so annoyed we'll need two ambulances!"

"So, you'll put up with her?"

"Guess I haven't got much choice. I'll send her to look for some obscure herb, and she'll get bored after a minute, sit down on a log and start brushing her hair. At least she'll be out of harm's way."

"Excellent."

"Thank you."

"Especially," continued Aunty Feng, "because you've started to combine face reading with common sense. That business about the nurse was nothing to do with the girl's face, but you still saw how important it was."

"It's not just common sense," I said. "It's more that I keep trying to turn things on their head to see if there's another side to the story."

"Excellent," said Aunty Feng.

"It is?"

"Yes," she grinned. "In China there are two sides to everything."

Yin and Yang

Moles on the skin are different to spots or scars, because they are always with you. They are not a part of your fate that can be avoided or dispelled. They will rule you from the time you are born until the day you die.

Human beings have two of everything down the sides and one of everything down the middle. Which is why we have one mouth and one nose, but two eyes and two ears. When we start talking about moles of course, it is very rare that one mole will be balanced by another in the same position on the other side of the face. For this reason, all that business about Yin and Yang *now* becomes very important, because the side of your face where the mole turns up will have a slightly different reading depending on whether it is Yin- or Yang-ruled. The Yin side of the face is the right side, and this rules intellect and intelligence. The Yang side of the face is the left side, which rules activity and strength. If anything turns up on a single side of the face, then you must think about what it means in terms of Yin and Yang.

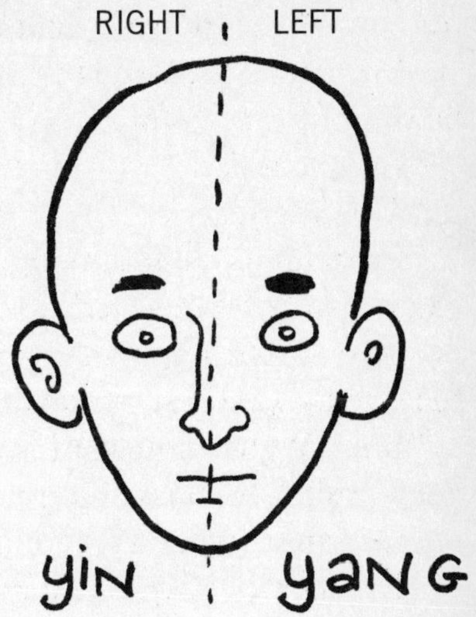

The Mark of Travel

If someone has a mole somewhere between their eyebrow and temple, they have a restless urge to wander. Their eyes look around trying to see the mole, but it's in one of those parts of the body that the eyes can't see. Instead, the constant looking around encourages the owner to seek out new places, and boldly go where no one has gone before. If anyone is a seasoned traveler, always jetting off to different

parts of the world, you'll find a travel mole somewhere near the outer edge of the person's eye. Whether the travel mole is in the Yin or Yang part of the face will determine why the person is always traveling. A Yang travel mole means the owner takes an active interest in getting out and about. They'll want to lead parties of explorers, or go foraging for food in the forest (when everyone else prefers to go to the supermarket). They'll permanently drop subtle hints by leaving new travel brochures lying around for all sorts of obscure destinations. Whether their parents like it or not, they will end up having a lot of weird holidays.

Their kids won't need any encouraging to get in the car or get on the plane. In fact, the kids will be the ones who are dragging the parents around.

However, if the mole is on the Yin side, the owner's traveling fate is far more passive. You may discover they have no interest in traveling and would rather stay at home watching television or reading a good book. But no matter how hard they try to put down roots and stay in one place, they are always dragged off on a new adventure. Quite possibly, their parents will have the kind of jobs that mean they have to move house often, or go to live in exotic places for long periods. Whatever the reason, these people will make a hideous mess of their friends' address books, because you can guarantee that the moment you write down their new address, you'll have to cross it out because they're on the move again.

The Mark of Tears

If someone has a mole under one eye, somewhere between the eye and the nose, there could be trouble. According to the Chinese, a woman who has a mole in the path of her tears is destined always to keep it fresh with weeping. Actually, it doesn't matter if you're a man or a woman, but the men don't like to admit that even they can get tearful from time to time.

The owner of a weeping mole can expect to be unlucky in love. Affairs of the heart will never seem to go right, but reading the face might give you a clue why. If the weeping mole is on the Yin side of the face, then the owner's love troubles will be passive in nature. They will allow their other half to wander, possibly even pay them too little attention. If they want to improve their fortunes in love, they should take a more active role, pay more attention to what's going on around them, and make more decisions for themselves, rather than leaving them in the hands of others.

However, if the weeping mole is on the other side of the face, in the Yang sector, then the owner's problems will stem from too much activity. They might be too possessive, make too many decisions without asking what their partner's opinion is, and be generally overbearing. If they want to try to turn their fate around, they should start thinking more of others' feelings, and stop assuming that everybody will do exactly as they are told.

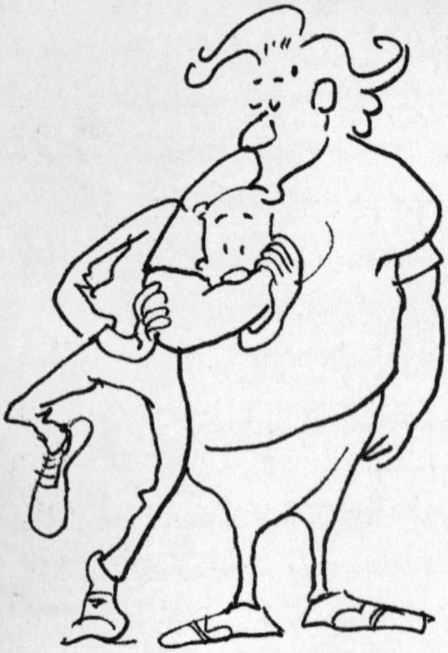

The Mark of Power

A mole on the upper area of the cheek is an indicator of authority. It draws attention to the powerful mountain of the cheekbone, itself a sign of leadership. If your cheekbones are particularly strong as well, this doubles your power to order other people around. There is a downside, which is the loneliness of command. Your destiny may place you at the head of the table or the front of the army, but when you turn to your left and right you may find you have nobody to talk to. A leader may be in charge, but can be so far ahead or so scary that they find themselves with very few real friends. Take care that you don't scare away your friends by being too commanding; some things are more important in life.

The location of a mole will tell us more about the nature of the power that the owner will enjoy, or possibly more about the way in which they can expect to lose their friends. If a mole is found on the right side of the face, it is in the Yin sector, and so the emphasis is on passivity. Authority will fall into the owner's lap, perhaps because they have a powerful family or have friends in high places. But passivity will also play a part in their friendships. They must not neglect their friends. It is often their friends who come calling on them, and never the opposite. One day the phone will stop ringing because their friends think they do not really care about them. They must prepare for this day, and hope to avoid it, by taking a more active interest in their friends' lives. Don't wait for others to come to you, make sure you show them how much you care.

If the mole is in the Yang sector, then the opposite applies. The owner will actively attain a position of power by going for it as if their life depended on it. They must be careful not to take their quest for power too seriously because they are the kind of person who, given half a chance, would sell their grandmother for extra pocket money and trip their friends up to get a better seat in class. They

should make sure they don't only talk to those people from whom they want a favor, otherwise the word will get around that they use people and are untrustworthy.

The Mark of Friendship

If the mole is further down the cheek, its meaning is very different. The *beauty spot* mole is a sign of a true friend and a great socialite. The owner of this mole will be at all the best parties, mixing with all the *in* crowds, surrounded by the most admirers and having the best time. But when they stagger home late at night, their parents will be standing by the door with their arms folded and faces like thunder. And this is where the problems start, because this mole has a dark side, too. Yes, the owner will be at all the best places with a huge group of great friends, but they might neglect their family. One day they will wake up and realize that they haven't spoken to their family for months, or even years, and that the people in the world who love them most might as well be complete strangers.

The Yin and Yang sectors of the face tell us how this might happen. If the mole is in the right (Yin) sector, it's likely to happen passively. The owner will be a kind of social butterfly, buffeted by pressures from other people. They may fall in with a crowd of people who encourage them to defy their parents, or may stay out longer than they should because their parents aren't much fun to be with. If the mole is in the left (Yang) sector, then it's harder to blame other people. It is the owner of the mole who decides to stay out too late, not caring that it might cause trouble; or who sneaks out of the house to see friends, whether or not the friends have invited them.

The Mark of Refinement

A mole on the upper lip, or just outside the upper lip, will draw attention to the mouth. Owners will have a great sense of taste and will appreciate fine foods and drinks. The mark of a true gourmet, this mole can also signify a greedy glutton if it grows too big.

If the mole is in the passive Yin sector on the right, the person will go to restaurants and friends' houses and savor every last morsel put before them. With luck, such a person is destined to be a food critic for a newspaper, and if unlucky, they might become a poison taster for a rich monarch. But if the mole is in the active Yang sector on the left, then the owner will take a much more active interest in the preparation of fine food. Instead of passing judgement on what others do, this person will want to learn how to actually do it. A fine future as a chef or restauranteur could be in store for them because, as far as they are concerned, the only way they can get hold of the best food is if they cook it themselves.

The Mark of Diplomacy

A mole on the outside corner of the chin brings mixed blessings. At first glance, especially if the light is wrong or you're not paying much attention, it can look exactly like a spot, since it turns up in the place where spots are most likely to grow. People might even assume that the owner doesn't wash as often as they should, or eats too much fatty food. However, to the Chinese face reader, this is actually a good thing, because it means the owner has to become very good at explaining themselves, and very good at forgiving the prejudices of others. While this mole might at first sight appear to be a disadvantage, it could turn the owner into an accomplished diplomat, able to get on with anybody.

Someone with a right (Yin) mole will go through life with ease. People will find them instantly likable. Wherever they go, others will want to be with them, and bitter rivals may even find they have something in common when they see that they have the same friend.

A left (Yang) placement means that the person is a more active sort of diplomat. They are good at getting people together and putting them at ease with one another. Investors with no projects and inventors with no money will meet each other at a Yang diplomat's party and thank their lucky stars that they have finally found someone who can help them. We, of course, know differently. Luck has nothing to do with it at all.

Owners of a Yang mole should be careful that they don't get used. They may be very good at introducing people to each other and smoothing over arguments, they may be great at hosting parties, but they may also have a number of hangers-on who make use their abilities and talents without really liking the person. Diplomacy is a great skill but even diplomats need real friends. Don't spend all your time making sure other people get along with each other. Remember who your real friends are.

The Marks of Success

One or more moles on the ears denote great fortune in the family and home. On the right (Yin) ear, moles mean passive success, which could mean winning the lottery, inheriting a huge mansion or having parents who set you up on a blind date with your future husband or wife who turns out to be royalty.

On the left (Yang) ear, moles mean active success, possibly building your own house, wooing the perfect spouse, or scrimping and saving successfully so that you can afford everything you need to make a cosy home. The downside, if you want to call it a downside, is that you will place the home and family before success in your career. If you are offered a great promotion which involves leaving your family behind for months on end, you are likely to turn it down because you care too much about them. You will live a long and fortunate life and have a happy old age surrounded by your great-grandchildren. Just don't expect to become the boss of a big company as well.

A mole in between the eyebrows is said by the Chinese to be a pearl, held by the twin dragons of the eyebrows. This means very great success indeed, especially in the political arena. The owner will lead a charmed life and is destined for great things.

A mole further up in the middle of the forehead is also a sign of success, although at a price. The owner will enjoy good fortune in business, politics, or school work, or possibly all three since they bear the mark of good fortune in all things. All things, that is, except love. If the mole is slightly to the right or left of center, that will give us a Yin or Yang explanation for their troubles. A passive (Yin) mole on the right means that the pursuit of other forms of success will leave the owner with little or no time to look for love. An active (Yang) mole on the left is perhaps even more tragic. Owners will have the chance to fall in love, but will be so busy with career or other plans that they will eventually scare the other person off.

The Mark of Children

A mole on the end of a man's nose is a sign that he will have many, many children. If he doesn't have any yet, he soon will, so you know that baby clothes and toys are always good birthday presents.

The Mark of Worry

A mole on the top of the forehead could mean trouble for its owner. Reaching up your hand to touch it looks as if you are scratching your head, which means you may set up a magic spell by *reminding* yourself all the time to be worried, concerned, and frustrated.

A mole on the right (Yin) means your worries will stem from leaving jobs undone and not taking an active interest in what others are planning.

A mole on the left (Yang) means that you are taking on more than you can handle. You should calm down and let others do more of the work, otherwise you will soon be blowing a fuse.

Freckles

Because freckles can come and go, they do not have the same power as moles. If a lone freckle appears in one of the mole sectors described above, just think of it as a minor development in that direction. Something the owner has done or is about to do will change their fortune in the direction indicated. Think of it as a warning, or an incentive, depending on whether or not you want the fortune that the freckle will bring.

Permanent freckles have a meaning of their own. Because they cluster and bustle all over the face, they look like a crowd of happy people at a party, and mean that someone is a friendly person, happiest when in a group.

Laughter Lines

Smile. Your cheeks will get chubbier because some of the skin will bunch up. Wrinkle your nose as well, and your cheeks will get even fatter. You will also see two lines going down the side of your face, starting on either side of the nose, curving out and down and eventually stopping somewhere around your mouth. These are your laughter lines, and are difficult to see when you are

young, but as you get older they will become clearer. In Chinese face reading, your laughter lines are your life lines, showing how long you can expect to live.

The best laughter lines to have are long, leisurely curves, shaped like a bell. If they reach down way past your mouth, then you can expect to live a very long time indeed. Most people, however, have laughter lines that only stretch as far as the mouth itself, which indicates an average, everyday threescore years and ten lifetime.

If the laughter lines curve inwards rather than outwards, this foretells loneliness in old age. If they curve in and actually meet with the edge of the mouth, then you'll have plenty of friends to keep you company while you sit by the fire, but none of you will have very much money.

Tramlines and Spamlines

We could fill an entire other book with stuff about the meanings of the lines on faces. Just like the lines on a person's palm, the lines on the face each have their own meaning and special message about destiny. But for you, this isn't all that important. You have a long wait until you have enough lines on your face worth reading, and as any adult will tell you, the longer you have to wait for a grizzled face, the better.

But as you get older, lines will start to appear, and they will probably become most obvious on your forehead. If you stare into a mirror and wiggle your eyebrows, you might just find the vague beginnings of lines on your forehead, known in the West as *worry lines*. In China, of course, there's more to them than that.

A Mind for Success

If you have a single line across your forehead, either high up or in the middle, then you have the potential to be a very successful person. If the line is lower down the forehead, closer to the eyebrows, then you run the risk of peaking too early. But no matter how successful you are now, don't think you can relax for the rest of your life. However fine the summer is, you must still prepare for the cold days of winter. This is a classic face reading for someone who enjoys great success at an early age, only to lose it all in an instant. A low line on the forehead could mean a career as a teenage rock star or supermodel. These may seem like dream jobs, but they are jobs with a sell-by date. Plan for the future, or it will take you by surprise.

Silver Linings

To the Chinese, the more lines on your forehead, the more intelligent you are. Two horizontal lines on the forehead are a sign of potential genius. Such a person likes to spend hours in deep thought, and should consider a career as an inventor, scientist, or philosopher.

Three horizontal lines is even more surprizing. To have that many dents in your face, you must have spent your early years wandering around in a state of extreme shock. The Chinese say this is a good thing, because it's a sign of someone who is endlessly saying, "I can't believe my luck!" The three lines on the forehead can be found in anyone who enjoys unbelievable good fortune. Pay very close attention to their decisions because these people are fated to win the lottery three times in a row, catch the crucial ball at the ball-game, and fluke their way through a charmed life. These people make invincible stuntmen and daredevil circus performers, but rarely need to work because they win so many prizes they can afford to put their feet up.

Freak Oblique

Some people may have single diagonal lines on their forehead, on either the left or the right side. They are particularly likely to occur if you are in the habit of raising a quizzical eyebrow every time someone does something stupid. Do it too often and you will etch a sideways groove above the offending eyebrow, and it will have an unpleasant effect on your fortune.

The slanting forehead line indicates trouble ahead in the owner's relationships with other human beings. As usual, the nature of the trouble will depend on which side of the face the line is. On the Yin (right) side, it shows too much passivity, an unwillingness to stand up and be counted when trouble starts. This kind of person will raise an eyebrow in disgust and walk on by. They risk losing their friends because they rarely lift a finger to help, even when those they love are in dire need.

If the slant is on the Yang (left) side of the face, the owner of it has the opposite problem. Far from being too lazy, this person will often take a role that is too active. They must be careful not to be over-critical of their friends and colleagues, or they may scare everyone away by constantly going on about how they could do a much better job.

Face Value

- ☺ Remember, there are two sides to every story. A beautiful face doesn't necessarily mean a beautiful person, it might mean vanity and selfishness. Always ask yourself what the downside could be, even of something that looks as if it benefits everyone.
- ☺ Also look for the upside of everything. Just because something looks like bad news, it doesn't mean it is. Every cloud has a silver lining.
- ☺ The right side of your face is Yin, and rules everything that is done to you. The left side of your face is Yang, and rules everything that you do to others.
- ☺ A mole or line in one of those areas means a change in fortune.

Face Facts: Moles and Lines

FACE FEATURE: MOLES	READING
Mole outside outer tip of eyebrow	Travel (like it or not)
Weeping mole (below eye)	Miserable love life
Mole on upper cheek	Power without friendship
Mole on lower cheek	Friends without family
Mole outside upper lip	Gourmet or glutton
Mole outside corner of chin	Diplomat and survivor
Moles on ears	Success without career
Mole between eyebrows	Great success
Mole in middle of forehead	Success without love
Mole on end of nose	Children
Mole at top of forehead	Frustration
Freckles	Friendly/flirty

LAUGHTER LINES	READING
Slightly curved lines	Average
Bell-shaped, ending below mouth	Very long life
Long but curved inwards	Long life but lonely old age
Curved into mouth	Long life but poverty

LINES ON FOREHEAD	READING
Horizontal forehead line	Success
Horizontal forehead line (low down)	Limit to success (check left/right)
2 horizontal forehead lines	Potential genius
3 horizontal forehead lines	Extreme good luck
Oblique line to the left	Yang limitations
Oblique line to the right	Too passive

Face to Face

Someone has a horizontal forehead line, a mole on the end of his nose, several moles on his ears, a big bulbous nose with small nostrils, and Number One eyebrows. Predict his ideal career.

CHAPTER 10

The Palaces of Fortune

"Is this another trick question?" I asked.

"Of course," said Aunty Feng.

"OK," I said. "The forehead line means success, the nose mole means children, the big nose means rich but the little nostrils means thrifty. And the Number One eyebrows mean he's well-organized. But there's a problem with the moles on the ears."

"Why's that?"

"Because that means he won't want a career. He won't want to leave home. He'd much rather—"

"Yes?"

"He'd much rather stay at home, look after the kids and do the housework while his wife goes to the office."

"Is that so unusual?"

"Well... no. Just—"

"Unexpected?"

"Yes. So, the answer is homemaker. Or househusband, whatever the word is. He's good with money, he'll stretch the family budget, and he loves keeping the home clean and cooking the dinner for everyone."

"Well done. See, it all makes sense. But you must pay attention when you read a fortune. Sometimes the answer is unexpected, even though it's staring you in the face!"

"Yes, it is all making sense," I admitted grudgingly.

"Good," said Aunty Feng, fluttering her fan.

"Except—" I began, and she shot me a look like thunder.

"Except *what*?" she growled.

"Except some of what you've said doesn't really work."

Aunty Feng made sputtering noises like a coffee percolator. One of her long eyebrows raised ever-so-slightly in a questioning look, and I knew I had to talk fast.

"Well," I continued. "You've told me about lines and moles and eyes and ears and all that.

"Yes."

"But what about spots? Scars? Bits of food? All those things that come and go. Like cold sores that keep on coming back to haunt you for ages?"

There was a long, long pause, while Aunty Feng studied me carefully.

"I'll tell you if you want," she said. "But I'm warning you now, this is where things get complicated."

"Why?" I asked.

"Gong!" she replied, and I sneaked a look behind me for men in white coats.

Out, Damn Spot

In the same way that feng shui divides your house into sectors ruling Wealth, Career, and so on, face reading divides up the human face. Different parts of the face rule different parts of your life. We're not born with scars, and spots, blemishes, and pimples come and go, but they all tell us how ill or healthy a particular part of someone's life must be. Spots may look horrible, but they can be very useful. They act like radar blips to warn of hazards in the future.

This is the point where face reading becomes really complicated, because the evidence is less easy to interpret. It's not like the basic features, where you can say with a single glance, "Aha! Huge nostrils, you're a big spender." You have to weigh the evidence and decide exactly which part of the fortune you are looking at.

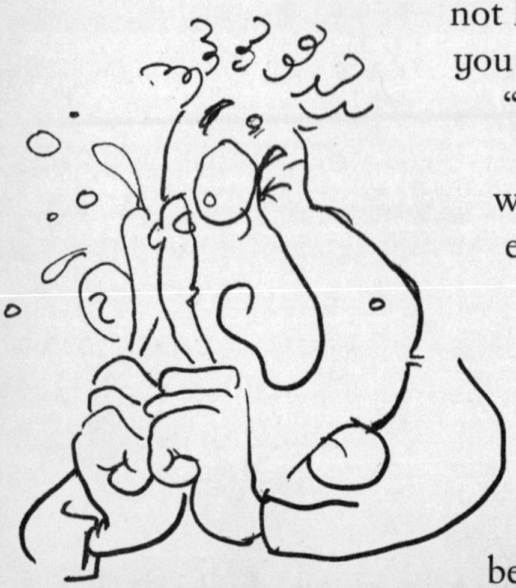

Let's say you suddenly develop a huge, glow-in-the-dark spot on the tip of your nose. This means financial trouble ahead, because the nose rules Wealth.

Something you've just done will badly affect your finances, but because we know this, we can do something about it. Take your savings out from under the mattress, cancel that investment in lunar energy, take back that expensive dress you couldn't afford, undo whatever money-related thing you have done in the last couple of days and, hey presto, the spot will fade away.

What we don't know, of course, is exactly what someone else has done to bring a spot upon themselves. As a face reader, you must talk this over with the owner of the spot.

Try not to give too much information away in the questions, because people have a habit of supplying information to fit whatever you ask them. If you immediately say, "Hmm, something financial… Have you bought anything recently?" they'll jump up and shout, "Yes! That's uncanny! Only yesterday I bought a milkshake! How did you know? This Chinese face reading is incredible!" But as they're running outside to tell the world about your mysterious talent for reading minds, they'll realize that you haven't actually done anything. You might as well have asked them if they put their pants on this morning.

You have to be more subtle. While you're looking at their face, measuring their ears and so on, get them to talk about the things they've been doing recently. This should give you a few clues about what changes they have made to their life which may affect their fate. If they've spent a lot of money on something, they're bound to mention it. They might have booked a holiday, started a new job, or lent a friend some money. If they've done it within a couple of days of the spot appearing, there's a chance that you've found the problem.

The human mind exerts a strange control over the body. Sometimes, the body and face speak where the brain is silent. They can tell us about a person's deep, hidden worries. Let's suppose the owner has lent someone some money. Deep down inside, they doubt whether they'll ever see it again. They might not want to admit it (perhaps they've lent it to their brother and don't want to cause any trouble in the family), but these worries will come out somehow. And who's to say they won't come out as a spot? Frustration, pain, anger, and doubt are all bad for a person's *qi*. Their blood will boil, their bile will rise, and this will create impurities and bad *qi* inside the body. The human body doesn't want bad *qi* inside it any longer than it has to, so it will push it out through the skin. It's your job to work out why it pushes its way out at that particular point.

These points are called *gong*, which is the Chinese word for palace. Whatever the face reading in the rest of the face, it is the palaces that are the most important areas. We have already hinted at some of the gong earlier in this book. For example, you already know that the nose is important for understanding someone's behavior with wealth. Well, here are the others.

Palaces of Fortune

GONG POINTS	RELATES TO
EYES	Intelligence
Under the eyes	Children
Outer tips of eyes	Marriage
EARS	Potential/Career
NOSE	Wealth/Business acumen
MOUTH	Personality/Sociability
EYEBROWS	Wisdom/Emotional state
FOREHEAD	Education
Left/Yang forehead	Father and his family
Right/Yin forehead	Mother and her family
Lower left forehead	Friends
Lower right forehead	Brothers/Sisters
TEMPLES	Travel
CHEEKBONES	Leadership
JAWBONE	Fame
CHIN	Strength
LAUGH LINES	Longevity
HAIR	Energy

Some palaces will appear twice, once on each side of the face, so remember that Yin and Yang will play an important part in determining the nature of the change in fortune. A new blemish on the chin means trouble with a person's strength, but if it is on the right side it is a Yin (passive) fortune. This means somebody has done something to the person which has changed their fortune. If it is on the left side it is an Yang fortune. This means the person has actively done something that will change his or her fortune. The nature of the blemish will also give you a few hints about the change in fortune.

Spots will fade away. If you get a spot, you can do something about it. But a scar may well stay with you forever, so it suggests a much more radical alteration to your fate and future. If you get a nasty cut on your face, it will only fade away entirely if you can undo the damage that has been done to your fortune.

Face Facts

- ☺ Different parts of your face rule different parts of your life.
- ☺ Blemishes in a particular area tell you where to expect trouble.
- ☺ Yin (right side) means trouble brought by others.
- ☺ Yang (left side) for trouble brought by your own actions.
- ☺ When it comes to predicting people's future, the more you know about them, the easier it is to see where they are going. Get them talking and see what their aims are in life. Where do they want to go? What do they want to do? How do they get on with other people? Once you have discovered their ambitions, use face reading to see if they will succeed.

Face to Face

You wake up one day and there's a huge, yellow spot on the lower right side of your forehead. As if that isn't bad enough, there's another one on your right temple. What could it mean?

CHAPTER 11

Facing the Future

"I don't know," I said. "I just don't know."

"Give it a try," said Aunty Feng.

"Well, lower right forehead means brothers or sisters, and right temple means trouble in travel, brought by somebody else's actions."

"Which means?"

"Well, that's the problem, without more information, I really have no idea. Maybe my brother has borrowed my bike, so I won't be able to get to the movies tonight. Maybe he's had a accident, and the bad luck is his. Maybe I'm going to have to go somewhere because of him and it's going to be a terrible journey. Maybe I'll have to walk home from somewhere because he's stolen my bus fare."

"Right."

"But," I protested. "It might be any of those things or

none of them. Real life isn't as simple as one of your little tests."

"That's right," said Aunty Feng. "And that's why you must always look for clues in the real world. Face reading might give you plenty of clues, but it'll never answer as many questions as common sense. Use face reading, but also use your eyes and ears and brain. If you knew where your brother was right now, you might get a better idea of what the spots on your face meant."

"Look for clues all around?"

"Yes," said Aunty Feng.

"Like the kite in the wind?"

"That's right," she said with a smile.

I turned to see how the girls in the park were getting on with their kite-flying, but they'd hit a snag. The kite was stuck in the branches of a tree and although it wasn't very far up, they were both too small to reach it.

"Don't just stand there," whispered Aunty Feng.

I reluctantly tramped over and got it down for them. They shouted, "Thank you!" to me as they ran out of the park. It was getting dark and everybody else had gone home.

I turned back to the bench, but Aunty Feng was gone.

In her place was a beautiful lady in a silk dress, who was just getting to her feet as I approached.

"Er..." I said.

"Yes, dear?" she said in a warm, silky voice. I could feel my knees turning to jelly.

"Have you seen a—?" I said, breathless. She was so beautiful I could hardly speak, with those long, almond-

shaped eyes and those sweeping eyebrows Aunty Feng had mentioned. Phoenix Eyes, that was what they were called.

"An old lady?" she asked with a smile that could melt icebergs.

I nodded dumbly.

"She had to go," said the beautiful woman. "She said she'll see you soon."

"But—" I said.

"But nothing," she smiled, gently wafting a fan across her face.

"Are you—?" I began. "That is— Were you—? Er..."

"Can't stay around here all day," she said, setting her fan down on the bench. "I have to get home."

"Er..." I tried again, unsuccessfully.

"And so should you, dear," she added.

"You're her, aren't you?" I said. "You're an old lady... Or was she *you* all along?"

"You tell me," she smiled. "You can't *always* judge by appearances."

"But—" I stammered.

"Must fly," she said, and with that she wafted down the path towards the distant trees.

The twilight was playing tricks with my eyes. I could have sworn she lifted up into the air and disappeared.

Just then, the lamps flickered on all across the park, and by the time my eyes had adjusted, there was nobody there but me.